Henry I. King

Races for the America's Cup

Henry I. King

Races for the America's Cup

ISBN/EAN: 9783337427832

Printed in Europe, USA, Canada, Australia, Japan

Cover: Foto ©Andreas Hilbeck / pixelio.de

More available books at **www.hansebooks.com**

Races for the America's Cup.

A HISTORY OF EACH OF THE INTER-
NATIONAL YACHT RACES FROM THE
BEGINNING

WITH ILLUSTRATIONS OF THE YACHTS,

TERMS OF THE RACES, ETC.

ALSO

The Cup Defenders of 1893.

——— By The New-York Tribune ———

THE AMERICA'S C[

CONTENTS.

INDEX.

THE RACES FOR THE AMERICA'S CUP.

Eight Spirited Contests.—American Yachts, the Swiftest in the World.—Preparations for the Race of 1893, the Ninth of the Series.

FIRST DEED OF GIFT.

NEW-YORK, July 8, 1857.

To the Secretary of the New-York Yacht Club:

SIR:—The undersigned, members of the New-York Yacht Club, and late owners of the Schooner Yacht "America," beg leave through you to present to the Club the Cup won by the "America" at the Regatta of the Royal Yacht Squadron at Cowes, England, August 22, 1851.

This Cup was offered as a prize to be sailed for by yachts of all nations, without regard to difference of tonnage, going round the Isle of Wight (the usual course for the Annual Regatta of the Royal Yacht Squadron), and was won by the "America," beating eight cutters and seven schooner yachts, which started in the race.

The Cup is offered to the New-York Yacht Club, subject to the following conditions:

Any organized yacht club of any foreign country shall always be entitled, through any one or more of its members, to claim the right of sailing a match for this cup with any yacht or other vessel of not less than thirty or more than three hundred tons, measured by the Custom House rule of the country to which the vessel belongs.

The parties desiring to sail for the Cup may make any match with the yacht club in possession of the same, that may be determined upon by mutual consent; but in case of disagreement as to terms, the match shall be sailed over the usual course for the annual regatta of the yacht club in possession of the Cup, and subject to the rules and sailing regulations—the challenging party being bound to give six months' notice in writing, fixing the day they wish to start. This notice to embrace the length, Custom House measurement, rig and name of the vessel.

It is to be distinctly understood that the Cup is to be the property of the Club, and not of the members thereof, or owners of the vessel winning it in a match; and that the condition of keeping it open to be sailed for by yacht clubs of all foreign countries, upon the terms above laid down, shall forever attach to it, thus making it perpetually a Challenge Cup for friendly competition between foreign countries.

> J. C. STEVENS,
> EDWIN A. STEVENS,
> HAMILTON WILKES,
> J. BEEKMAN FINLEY,
> GEORGE L. SCHUYLER.

On motion of Mr. Grinnell, it was

Resolved, That the New-York Yacht Club accept the Cup won by the "America," and presented to them by the proprietors, upon the terms and conditions appointed by them.

Resolved, That the letter of Mr. Schuyler, with the enclosure, be entered on the minutes, and the Secretary be requested to furnish to all foreign yacht clubs a copy of the conditions upon which this Club holds the Cup, and which permanently attach to it.

> N. BLOODGOOD, Secretary.

SECOND DEED OF GIFT.

NEW-YORK, January 4, 1882.

To the Secretary of the New-York Yacht Club:

DEAR SIR:—I have to acknowledge the receipt of your letter of December, 17, 1881, enclosing the resolutions of the New-York Yacht Club of the date, and also the return of the "America's" Cup to me, as the survivor of the original donors.

I fully concur with the views expressed in the resolutions, that the deed of gift, made so many years ago, is, under present circumstances, inadequate to meet the intentions of the donors, and too onerous upon the Club in possession, which is required to defend it against all challengers.

As the New-York Yacht Club, by your communication and under the resolutions themselves, express a desire to be again placed in possession of the Cup under new conditions, I have conferred with the Committee appointed at the meeting and have prepared a new deed of gift of this Cup as a perpetual Challenge Cup. It is hoped that, as regards both challenging and challenged parties, its terms will be considered just and satisfactory to organized Yacht Clubs of all countries.

There is one clause which may require explanation. Owing to the present and increasing size of ocean steamers, it would be quite feasible for an American, English or French Club to transport on their decks yachts of large tonnage. This might be availed of in such a way that the match would not be a test of sea-going qualities as well as of speed, which would essentially detract from the interest of a national competition.

The "America's" Cup is again offered to the New-York Yacht Club, subject to the following conditions:

Any organized Yacht Club of a foreign country, incorporated, patented or licensed by the Legislature, Admiralty or other executive department, having for its annual regatta an ocean water course on the sea or on an arm of the sea (or one which combines both), practicable for vessels of 300 tons, shall always be entitled, through one or more of its members, to the right of sailing a match for this Cup, with a yacht or other vessel propelled by sails only, and constructed in the country to which the challenging Club belongs, against any one yacht or vessel as aforesaid, constructed in the country of the Club holding the Cup.

The yacht or vessel to be of not less than 30 nor more than 300 tons, measured by the Custom House rule in use by the country of the challenging party.

The challenging party shall give six months' notice in writing, naming the day for the proposed race, which day shall not be less than seven months from the date of the notice.

The parties intending to sail for the Cup may, by mutual consent, make any arrangement satisfactory to both as to date, course, time allowance, number of trials, rules and sailing regulations, and any and all other conditions of the match, in which case also the six months' notice may be waived.

In case the parties cannot mutually agree upon the terms of a match, then the challenging party shall have the right to contest for the Cup in one trial, sailed over the usual course of the Annual Regatta of the Club holding the Cup, subject to its rules and sailing regulations, the challenging party not being required to name its representative until the time agreed upon for the start.

Accompanying the six months' notice, there must be a Custom House certificate of the measurement, and a statement of the dimensions, rig and name of the vessel.

No vessel which has been defeated in a match for this Cup can be again selected by any club for its representative, until after a contest for it by some other vessel has intervened, or until after the expiration of two' years from the times such contest has taken place.

Vessels intending to compete for the Cup must proceed under sail on their own bottoms to the port where the contest is to take place.

Should the Club holding the Cup be, for any cause, dissolved, the Cup shall be handed over to any club of the same nationality it may select, which comes under the foregoing rules.

It is to be distinctly understood that the Cup is to be the property of the Club and not of the owners of the vessel winning it in a match, and that the conditions of keeping it open to be sailed for by organized yacht clubs of all foreign countries, upon the terms above laid down, shall forever attach to it, thus making it perpetually a Challenge Cup for friendly competition between foreign countries.

GEORGE L. SCHUYLER.

THIRD DEED OF GIFT.

SECRETARY'S OFFICE,
67 MADISON AVENUE,
NEW-YORK, Oct. 28, 1887.

SIR:—I am directed to inform the members of your (Foreign Yacht Club's) Association that the One Hundred Guinea Cup, won by the Yacht America, at Cowes, England, August 22, 1851, at the Regatta of the Royal Yacht Squadron, as a prize offered to yachts of all nations, having been returned to Mr. George L. Schuyler, the only surviving donor, has been re-conveyed to the New-York Yacht Club by the following deed of gift:

This Deed of Gift, made the twenty-fourth day of October, one thousand eight hundred and eighty-seven, between George L. Schuyler, as sole surviving owner of the Cup won by the Yacht America, at Cowes, England, on the twenty-second day of August, one thousand eight hundred and fifty-one, of the first part, and the New-York Yacht Club, of the second part, witnesseth:

That the said party of the first part, for, and in consideration of the premises and of the performance of the conditions and agreements hereinafter set forth by the party of the second part, has granted, bargained, sold, assigned, transferred, and set over, and by these presents does grant, bargain, sell, assign, transfer and set over, unto the said party of the second part, its successors and assigns, the Cup won by the Schooner Yacht America, at Cowes, England, upon the twenty-second day of August, 1851. To have and to hold the same to the said party of the second part, its successors and assigns, IN TRUST, NEVERTHELESS, for the following uses and purposes:

This Cup is donated upon the condition that it shall be preserved as a perpetual Challenge Cup for friendly competition between foreign countries.

Any organized Yacht Club of a foreign country, incorporated, patented or licensed by the Legislature, Admiralty or other executive department, having for its annual regatta an ocean watercourse on the sea, or on an arm of the sea, or one which combines both, shall always be entitled to the right of sailing a match for this Cup, with a yacht or vessel propelled by sails only, and constructed in the country to which the Challenging Club belongs, against any one yacht or vessel constructed in the country of the Club holding the Cup.

The competing yachts or vessels, if of one mast, shall be not less than sixty-five feet, nor more than ninety feet on the load water line; if of more than one mast, they shall be not less than eighty feet, nor more than one hundred and fifteen feet on the load water line.

The Challenging Club shall give ten months' notice in writing, naming the days for the proposed races; but no races shall be sailed in the days intervening between November first and May first. Accompanying the ten months' notice of challenge, there must be sent the name of the owner and a certificate of the name, rig and following dimensions of the challenging vessel, namely: length on load water line; beam at load water line, and extreme beam; and draught of water; which dimensions shall not be exceeded; and a Custom House registry of the vessel must also be sent as soon as possible. Vessels selected to compete for this Cup must proceed under sail, on their own bottoms, to the port where the contest is to take place. Centreboard or sliding keel vessels shall always be allowed to compete in any race for this Cup, and no restriction nor limitation whatever shall be placed upon the use of such centreboard or sliding keel, nor shall the centreboard or sliding keel be considered a part of the vessel for any purposes of measurement.

The Club challenging for the Cup and the Club holding the same, may, by mutual consent, make any arrangements satisfactory to both as to the dates, courses, number of trials, rules and sailing regulations, and any and all other conditions of the match, in which case also the ten months' notice may be waived.

In case the parties cannot mutually agree upon the terms of a match, then three races shall be sailed and the winner of two of such races shall be entitled to the Cup. All such races shall be on ocean courses, free from headlands, as follows: The first race, twenty nautical miles to windward and return; the second race, an equilateral triangular race of thirty-nine nautical miles; the first side of which shall be a beat to windward; the third race (if necessary) twenty nautical miles to windward and return; and one week day shall intervene between the conclusion of one race and the starting of the next race.

These ocean courses shall be practicable in all parts for vessels of twenty-two feet draught of water, and shall be selected by the Club holding the Cup; and these races shall be sailed subject to its rules and sailing regulations so far as the same do not conflict with the provisions of this deed of gift, but without any time allowance whatever. The Challenged Club shall not be required to name its representative vessel until at the time agreed upon for the start, but the vessel when named must compete in all the races; and each of such races must be completed within seven hours.

Should the Club holding the Cup be for any cause dissolved, the Cup shall be transferred to some Club of the same nationality, eligible to challenge under this deed of gift, in trust and subject to its provisions. In the event of the failure of such transfer within three months after such dissolution, said Cup shall revert to the preceding Club holding the same, and under the terms of this deed of gift. It is distinctly understood that the Cup is to be the property of the Club subject to the provisions of this deed, and not the property of the owner or owners of any vessel winning a match.

No vessel which has been defeated in a match for this Cup can be again selected by any Club as its representative vessel until after a contest for it by some other vessel has intervened, or until after the expiration of two years from the time of such defeat. And when a challenge from a Club fulfilling all the conditions required by this instrument has been received, no other challenge can be considered until the pending event has been decided.

AND the said party of the second part hereby accepts the said Cup, subject to the said trust, terms and conditions, and hereby covenants and agrees to and with said party of the first part, that it will faithfully and fully see that the foregoing conditions are fully observed and complied with by any contestant for the said Cup during the holding thereof by it; and that it will assign, transfer and deliver the said Cup to the foreign Yacht Club whose representative yacht shall have won the same in accordance with the foregoing terms and conditions, provided the said foreign Club shall by instrument in writing, lawfully executed, enter with said party of the second part into the like covenants as are herein entered into by it, such instrument to contain a like provision for the successive assignees to enter into the same covenants with their respective assignors, and to be executed in duplicate, one to be retained by each Club, and a copy thereof to be forwarded to the said party of the second part.

In Witness Whereof, The said party of the first part has hereunto set his hand and seal, and the said party of the second part has caused its corporate seal to be affixed to these presents and the same to be signed by its Commodore and attested by its Secretary, the day and year first above written.

In the presence of
H. D. HAMILTON.
   GEORGE L. SCHUYLER, (L. S.)
    The New-York Yacht Club.
  By ELBRIDGE T. GERRY, Commodore.
   JOHN H. BIRD, Secretary.
(Seal of New-York Yacht Club).

The New-York Yacht Club, having accepted the gift, with the conditions above expressed, consider this a fitting occasion to present the subject to the Yacht Clubs of all nations, and invokes from them a spirited contest for the Championship, and trusts that it may be the source of continued friendly strife between the institutions of this description throughout the world, and therefore requests that this communication may be laid before your members at their earliest meeting, and earnestly invites a friendly competition for the possession of the prize, rendering to any gentleman who may favor it with a visit, and who may enter into the contest, a liberal, hearty welcome, and the strictest fair play.

    Respectfully,
    Your obedient servant,
     JOHN H. BIRD,
   Secretary of the New-York Yacht Club.

———

At a meeting of the New-York Yacht Club, held on the 17th day of May, 1888, the following preamble and resolution respecting the new deed of gift of the "America's" Cup were unanimously adopted:

"WHEREAS, the Secretary of this Club has received letters, dated November 26, 1887, from the Royal London Yacht Club and from the Yacht Racing Association, representing the principal yacht clubs of Europe, and dated February 22, 1888, regretting that the terms of the new deed of gift of the 'America's' Cup, presented by George L. Schuyler, and dated October 28, 1887, are such that foreign vessels are unable to challenge ; and, whereas, in this deed of gift, by which the Cup is now held by this Club, any mutual agreement may be made between the challenged and challenging party; therefore

"Resolved, That the terms under which the races between 'Genesta' and 'Puritan,' 'Galatea' and 'Mayflower,' and 'Thistle' and 'Volunteer' were sailed, are considered satisfactory to this Club, and a challenge under these terms would be accepted, but with the positive understanding that if the Cup is won by the Club challenging, it shall be held under and subject to the full terms of the new deed, dated October 28, 1887, inasmuch as this Club believes it to be in the interest of all parties, and the terms of which are distinct, fair and sportsmanlike."

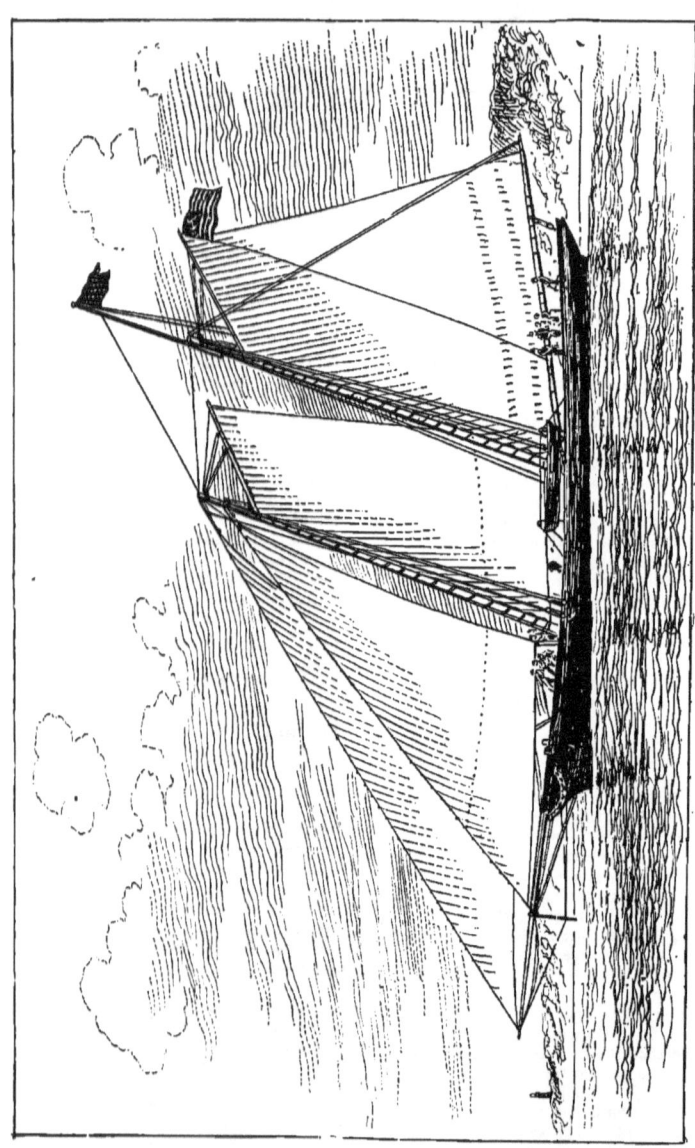

THE CELEBRATED YACHT "AMERICA."

Winner of the "Queen's Cup," Value 100 Guineas, in the Royal Yacht Squadron Match for all Nations, at Cowes, England, August 22, 1851,

HOW THE CUP WAS FIRST WON

THE AMERICA'S FAMOUS RACE ABROAD.

SHE LEFT THE WHOLE BRITISH YACHTING
FLEET BEHIND HER—SUPERIOR WORK
OF THE AMERICAN CREW.

The first race for the America's Cup was sailed
around the Isle of Wight on August 22, 1851.
Of the yachts which sailed the seas then the
America is probably the only one now in commission, and of participants and spectators the
larger number have joined the silent majority.
The Royal Yacht Squadron had offered a cup
open to competition by yachts of all nations.

the start was given. The yachts which started
were Sir W. P. Carew's schooner Beatrice, 161
tons; the Duke of Marlborough's schooner Wy-
vern, 205 tons; the Marquis of Conyngham's
schooner Constance, 218 tons; Sir H. B. Hugh-
ton's schooner Gypsy Queen, 160 tons; Lord A.
Paget's cutter Mona, eighty-two tons; J. L.
Cragie's cutter Volante, forty-eight tons; A. Hill's
schooner Ione, seventy-five tons; T. Chamber-
layne's cutter Arrow, eighty-four tons; J. Weld's
cutter Alarm, 193 tons; G. H. Acker's schooner
Brilliant, a three-master of 392 tons; B. H. Jones's
cutter Bacchante, eighty tons; W. Curling's
cutter Freak, sixty tons; H. S. Fearon's cutter
Eclipse, fifty tons; T. Le Merchant's cutter
Aurora, forty-seven tons, and the America, which
was put down on the entry list as of 170 tons.
The America was the last yacht to get off.

THE AMERICA CROSSING THE OCEAN UNDER PILOT RIG

The regatta for it was set for August 22. The
America was lying at Cowes, and her owners
were anxious to get a match race with a representative British yacht. All challenges, public
and private, however, were met by the Englishmen with a reference to the regatta of August
22. Commodore Stevens decided to enter, as he
could get no other race, and so on that memo-
rable day he sailed against the British fleet and
won the trophy. The course from Cowes around
the Isle of Wight, over which the race was
sailed, is one where currents and tides contend
and is as unfair to a stranger as is the old inside
course of the New-York Yacht Club in the
Lower Bay. Happily international races are now
sailed on the open sea.

THE YACHTS WHICH STARTED.

The wind was blowing lightly from the west
that morning, when at 10 o'clock the signal for

She ran wing and wing, her mainsail out on one
side and her foresail on the other, and soon
passed through all of the fleet except the leading
boats, which were Beatrice, Aurora, Volante and
Arrow. Finally the America, by a good deal
of dodging to avoid furling, managed to get past
these leading boats. The breeze was freshening
steadily, and by the time No Man's Land buoy
was turned it was blowing a good six-knot breeze.
The Yankee boat, with the wind free, had done
just what had been expected by her owners and
feared by the English, and shown her great superiority over her competitors.

EXCELLENT WINDWARD WORK.

Now when it came to windward work she
proved that she was equally proficient, and soon
was a good distance ahead of the nearest yacht
and two miles to windward of her. She worked
to windward so speedily that by the time the

Point was reached there was not a yacht in sight from her decks. The wind now died down, and a strong head tide was encountered, against which the America made little headway. This gave the fleet, which had not yet caught the full strength of the tide, a chance to crawl up on her. The little cutter Aurora and the cutter Arrow nearly caught up with the America, though the rest of the fleet was still a safe distance astern.

At St. Catherine's the Arrow went aground and was out of the race, but the little Aurora still held on, and, her size considered, did excellently with the America. The wind now began to freshen again, and the America drew rapidly away from the cutter. After getting by St. Catherine's the America had a leading wind, and easing off her sheets flew rapidly up toward Cowes. The America had gone over under pilotboat rig, or as pilotboats were rigged in those days, and had no foretopmast and no jibboom until just before the race. Before the race she had a jibboom fitted so that she could carry a flying jib. Just before passing St. Catherine's her jibboom carried away, much to the satisfaction of "Old Dick" Brown, her sailing master, who did not believe in a flying jib for windward work.

CLEARING AWAY THE JIBBOOM.

The America had a large and well-trained crew on board, and the wreckage was speedily cleared away. By the time the America passed the Needles, those waveworn rocks which guard the western entrance to the Solent and Southampton waters, the nearest boat, the Aurora, was about eight miles astern, and the rest of the fleet not in sight. The wind now became light again, and though the America passed the Needles at 5:40 o'clock, it was 8:37 o'clock before she dropped her anchor, a winner, off the Royal Yacht Club's castle at Cowes. The Aurora got in at 8:55 o'clock. The America's time in the race was 10 hours 37 minutes.

The only bet made on the race which has come down in history was one made by Henry Steers, the designer of the America, with Ratsey, a celebrated yacht builder in those days. Ratsey made the new jibboom for the America, and bet him the price of the spar that the America would be beaten.

The defeated fleet of British yachts did not all get in until the day after the race. Many of them became discouraged and anchored where night overtook them. The America was well handled throughout the race. From start to finish she showed her superiority over the British yachts in every respect. After the race G. H. Ackers, the owner of the three-masted schooner Brilliant, entered a protest against the cup being given to the America on the ground that she had passed on the wrong side of the Nab Light. It was found, however, that the sailing directions given to Commodore Stevens contained no instructions regarding the side the light was to be left on, and the protest was disallowed. George R. Schuyler, who was the last to die of the original owners of the America, and who was aboard the yacht the day of the race, says, in a statement published in Coffin's "America's Cup" in 1885: "Had there been an allowance of time for tonnage, the Aurora, by Ackers's scale, would have been beaten by less than two minutes, although at one time eight miles astern; or had the drifting continued an hour or two longer it would have given her the cup—in which case I have no doubt the America's superiority, instead of being a national triumph, would have been confined to the knowledge of experts only."

FAME MUST HAVE COME TO HER.

As it was, however, the America gained the victory her superiority deserved and became famous forever. Had she not won the race at Cowes it is hardly probable that the obscurity referred to by Mr. Schuyler would ever have overtaken her. She showed from the first such immense superiority over the British fleet that Commodore Stevens would never have rested until he had demonstrated the excellencies of his boat to the world by some signal victory. The manner in which the America was handled in the race called forth praise from the observers. Before the start she had her sails down, but at the starting signal her nimble crew of American sailors set her mainsail, foresail, gaff-topsails and jib almost in an instant. One moment she was at anchor under bare poles, the next her clouds of canvas covered her and she was off for victory.

The year of the race of the America was the year of the Crystal Palace exhibit, and there was much racing at Cowes that season. The victory of the America was witnessed by a most distinguished company, the Queen, surrounded by noble lords and ladies and gentlemen in waiting, looking on at the start and finish from the battlements of the Royal Yacht Squadron's castle. There was no little dismay among the British yachtsmen at Cowes that night of August 22 when it spread about that the America had won. When the America had first appeared in British waters she was looked upon with indifference, and mildly contemptuous remarks were made at the presumption of the Yankees in thinking that they had a boat which could beat a crack British yacht. After she had hung about Cowes for a while and had had one or two impromptu brushes with yachts of the Royal Squadron, opinions began to change, and yachts were inclined to fight shy of the unprepossessing Yankee.

COMMODORE STEVENS'S EFFORTS.

Commodore Stevens tried his best to get a match race before the regatta of August 22 came off, but failed. He posted in the Royal Squadron's castle a challenge to sail the America against any British vessel whatever for from one thousand to ten thousand guineas in a six-knot breeze, and threw down the gauntlet to England, Ireland and Scotland. When the race for the Royal Squadron's Cup was over and the victory won the British yachtsmen did not attempt as a rule to deny that the America was the best boat of all those assembled at Cowes. There were a few pig-headed people, as there always are, who called the victory an accident, but every one who knew what he was talking about was convinced that a new era in shipbuilding had dawned. Some of the British yachtsmen while admitting the superiority of the America declared that they could build a boat in three months that would beat her. Commodore Stevens offered to stay over at Cowes for three months and wait for the boat to be built and race her for $125,000. This offer was not accepted.

On August 28 The America sailed a match race with Robert Stephenson's schooner Titania, of 100 tons, in heavy weather, and beat her nearly an hour. It took about twelve days in those times for a steamer to go from Liverpool to New-York, and the Atlantic cable had not joined the two worlds in daily conversation, so the fame of the victory of the America had spread over Great Britain and France before it reached her native shores. It got here, finally, however, and great was the satisfaction. The press of England, as a rule, gave the American schooner full credit for her performance, and called upon British yacht builders and British yachtsmen to be up and doing to regain their lost prestige. British yacht builders and British yachtsmen responded to the call, but an onward march, a march which has sometimes faltered, but always revived under the stimulus of international competition, began on this side the water in yacht building also, and so far the English have been unable to regain the prestige lost at Cowes in 1851.

A CONTEST OF THE BEST TYPES.

In that first race the America, which was undoubtedly the best production of yacht designing skill in this country at the time, sailed against not only one but several boats, which represented in their different types the best of British skill. The best of each nation came together, and the best of the Americans was proved beyond doubt to be better than the best of the British. The crew of the America also showed the British what American sailors were like, and impressed upon them the necessity of skill and discipline in yacht racing, a lesson which they learned rapidly and well. No yacht in the race at Cowes was handled so well as the America, so far as the crew was concerned.

The defeat of the British fleet was not pleasant to Englishmen, who do not take kindly to that sort of thing, but it was of great benefit and profit to them ultimately. After the race "The London Punch" published a cartoon representing two boys, John and Jonathan, sailing toy boats and Jonathan saying to John, "If you don't look sharp, I'll show you how to make a seventy-four next." The same paper contained a set of doggerel verses, in parody of "Yankee Doodle" and glorifying the victory of the America.

Thus was the America's cup first lost and won, and a great international trophy established for all time. As long as yachts shall sail the seas and yachtsmen love the swift rush of shapely hulls borne by canvas wings over tumbling seas, so long shall the memory of that first race at Cowes endure.

CAMBRIA'S VAIN EFFORTS.

HOW THE SECOND INTERNATIONAL YACHT RACE WAS WON.

THE ENGLISH BOAT HAD NO CHANCE FROM THE START—BEATEN BY HALF A FLEET.

The second race for the America's Cup was preceded by that preliminary correspondence which has ever since been apparently necessary to arrange a race for the trophy. The race was sailed in 1870, but the correspondence relating to it began in 1868.

James Ashbury, owner of the schooner yacht Cambria, was the challenger, as representative of the Royal Thames Yacht Club. The Cambria, it has been declared since, was not the fastest British schooner of the time, and her record in England gives weight to this claim. Still she was, if not the very fastest, at least a fair representative of British schooner yachts of the time, and the outcome proved that it did not take the fastest schooner yacht in America to beat her. She was beaten by yachts that were no more entitled to be called the fastest in America than she was to be considered the fastest in England, a point which Lord Dunraven appears to have overlooked in his article on international yachting in "The North American Review." The race was, after all that has been said, a fair international test, and, as usual, the Americans won.

This race of 1870 was the last one sailed for the cup where one boat sailed against a fleet, a manifestly unfair condition, but the one, nevertheless, under which the America won the cup in 1851. The cup, after having been won by the America, had been presented by her owners to the New-York Yacht Club to remain forever an international yachting trophy. The cup had become the absolute property of the owners of the America when that yacht won it, and they conveyed it to the New-York Yacht Club in trust under a "deed of gift" embodying the following conditions:

"Any organized yacht club of any foreign country shall always be entitled, through any one or more of its members, to claim the right of sailing a match for this cup with any yacht or other vessel of not less than thirty nor more than three hundred tons, measured by the custom house rule of the country to which the vessel belongs. The parties desiring to sail for the cup may make any match with the yacht club in possession of the same that may be determined upon by mutual consent; but in case of disagreement as to terms the match shall be sailed over the usual course for the annual regatta of the yacht club in possession of the cup, and subject to its rules and sailing regulations—the challenging party being bound to give six months' notice in writing, fixing the day they wish to start. This notice to embrace the length, custom house measurement, rig and name of the vessel. It is to be distinctly understood that the cup is to be the property of the club and not of the members thereof, or owners of the vessel winning it in a match, and that the condition of keeping it open to be sailed for by yacht clubs of all foreign countries upon the terms above laid down shall forever attach to it, thus making it perpetually a challenge cup for friendly competition between foreign countries."

Mr. Ashbury in his long correspondence with the New-York Yacht Club seemed to give rather a cold shoulder to the deed of gift, and, among other things regarded as rather unnecessary at the time and since, said he did not propose to put his boat against a "mere shell or racing machine." However, the match was finally arranged, and in July of 1870 the Cambria started for these shores in company with the schooner yacht Dauntless, then the property of James Gordon Bennett. It was a race over, and the Cambria won. The Dauntless led nearly all the way over, but at the Georges Banks, the wind shifting, she stood to the southward; the Cambria got a favorable slant of wind, cut inside of her and got by the lightship first. It was luck, and in subsequent races the

THE CAMBRIA.

Dauntless showed that she was the better boat, but, nevertheless, the Cambria won, and many people at that time thought she would win the race for the cup.

This being the first time a British yacht had crossed over here to race for the cup, there was great interest taken, not only in New-York, but throughout the country, in the coming contest. As Mr. Ashbury and the New-York Yacht Club were unable to agree upon terms of a race, it was decided to sail it, as the deed of gift directed in such cases, over the New-York Yacht Club course, and under the sailing regulations of that club.

The day set for the race was August 8, and everywhere the coming race was the talk of the town. The newspapers published columns about the approaching contest, and when finally it came off a great flotilla of boats of all kinds, crowded with people, went out to see it. So great was the interest in this race that the Government had fitted up the old America, then a training vessel at Annapolis, for racing, and put her in the fleet of yachts which was to defend the cup from the Cambria. The fleet of yachts selected to sail against the Cambria consisted of the keel schooners America, Dauntless, Rambler, Fleetwing, Restless, Tarolinta and

Alarm, and the centreboard schooners Phantom, Magic, Madgie, Silvie, Tidal Wave, Madeleine, Idler, Palmer, Alice, Fleur de Lis, Era, Josephine, Calypso, Widgeon, Halcyon and Jessie. The start was from an anchorage off Stapleton, and the course lay out around Sandy Hook Lightship and back to the starting point.

A good sailing breeze blew from the southeast and the water was smooth. The tide was running a strong ebb, and when the starting signal was given the yachts spread their canvas, tripped their anchors, and flew for the Narrows. They split tacks in all directions, and at first the bay was filled with such a number of swift-gliding craft running hither and thither that it was impossible to tell what yachts were in the lead. But it was soon seen that the Magic had the best of it and was getting a good lead. The newspaper accounts of the race that day describe her as remarkably quick in getting under way. She was the first of the fleet to get off and stood over toward the Long Island shore until she was able, by standing close in, to lay her course on the port tack down through the Narrows, fetching well down the West Bank. The America was the last to get off, but she soon took second place, with the Idler third and the Silvie fourth.

In working down the bay to the Southwest Spit all the fleet passed ahead of the Cambria except-ing the Tarolinta, Alice and Rambler. At the Southwest Spit buoy the order was as follows: Magic, America, Idler, Phantom, Dauntless, Madgie, Calypso, Halcyon, Fleetwing, Madeleine, Cambria, Tarolinta, Alice and Rambler. The other yachts before named had not started or had drawn out of the race. The Magic had got such a lead that it was evident, accidents barred, that nothing could catch her. As to the Cambria, she was a beaten boat already.

The yachts reached out by the point of the Hook against a flood tide, which had begun to run. Outside the Hook they stood a short distance to the southward and then reached for the light-ship. The Idler and Dauntless passed ahead of the America on the way out to the lightship, but the Cambria remained "in the ruck." The Magic rounded the lightship twenty-four minutes ahead of the Cambria, and between the British yacht and the leading boat at the turn there were six other schooners.

The run in from the lightship was one of the most beautiful sights from a spectacular point of view ever seen at a yacht race, all the schooners setting their light canvas and rushing over the sparkling waters, great double towers of white and wind-blown sails. The Cambria met an acci-dent as she ran in by the Point of the Hook, a sudden squall taking her foretopmast out of her. This, of course, made a difference in her showing at the end of the race as regards time, but not in the result as to the possession of the cup—that had been settled almost before the yachts had passed the Narrows.

The Cambria was quick in stays, had a large sail area and sailed close to the wind, but she did not sail fast enough. With that trifling ex-ception she was as good a boat as there was in the fleet. She was built by Ratsey, then a celebrated English yacht builder and the same who bet the price of the America's new jibboom in 1851 that the Yankee boat would not win the race against the Royal Yacht Squadron.

When the yachts rounded the Southwest Spit buoy on the run home the line of yachts had become so strung out that nearly three-quarters of an hour separated the Magic, still the leading boat, and the last boat of the fleet. The Idler, which was second when the lightship was rounded, now held third place, the Dauntless having passed ahead of her, and the old America was still fourth. The Cambria was eighth in the race at this point, the same position she occupied when the lightship was rounded. The yachts all made good time on the run in from the lightship, the Magic making the Southwest Spit in forty-five minutes and the Idler in forty-three minutes. The distance is about seven miles. The wind had been freshening, and with the strong breeze and the rapidly running flood-tide the yachts came up the bay in fast time. At the finish the Cambria was tenth. The Magic beat her thirty-nine minutes thirteen seconds on corrected time, and twenty-seven minutes three seconds on actual time. The America beat the Cambria thirteen minutes, forty-seven seconds on corrected time, and thirteen minutes three seconds on actual time. The order of the yachts at the finish was as follows: Magic, Idler, Silvie, Aimofrica, Dauntless, Madgie, Phantom, Alice, Halcyon, Cambria, Calypso, Fleetwing, Madeleine, Tarolinta and Rambler.

The cup was not at any time in danger, and it will be seen that there were several schooners in the fleet of the New-York Yacht Club which could outsail the Cambria on every point. It might be argued that the course sailed was one unfair to a stranger, in that part of it lay in the Lower Bay, where an intimate knowledge of tidal currents and local depths and shallows plays an important part in yacht racing. It will be observed, however, that the Cambria did no better outside Sandy Hook than she did in the bay, and in several matches which she sailed against American yachts on the open sea outside Newport subsequently she lost all except one. She did defeat the Idler once, but that was due entirely to an accident, the Idler parting her bobstay and being obliged to stand on a losing tack until it was repaired.

When the season was over Mr. Ashbury was thoroughly convinced that the Cambria was no match for the American schooners, so he went back to England and gave orders to Ratsey for a schooner which was to be built with the express design of winning the cup. This was the last race for the cup where a challenging yacht was called upon to sail against a fleet, it having become the general opinion among yachtsmen that, although the trophy had been won in that manner by the America, such a contest was not fair, and not in accordance with the spirit of the deed of gift. Three eminent judges and George L. Schuyler, the surviving giver of the cup, gave to the Commodore of the New-York Yacht Club an opinion, in which they construed the deed of gift to mean that one boat only should be put against a challenging yacht.

AN UNPLEASANT CHAPTER

THE LIVONIA'S ATTEMPT TO TAKE BACK THE AMERICA'S CUP.

TROUBLE MADE BY THE SECOND BRITISH CHALLENGER—TWO BOATS DEFENDED THE CUP—WORK OF THE COLUMBIA AND THE SAPPHO.

The second attempt of the British to win back the America's Cup is the most unpleasant part of the history of the great trophy. James Ashbury, who had been defeated the year before in his attempt to win the cup with the Cambria, challenged for it again in 1871 with a new schooner which he had built for the express purpose of winning the trophy. She was named the Livonia, and was built by Ratsey. She was built on scientific principles, as they were understood in those days, and the English papers in speaking of her declared "it had at last been discovered just what the water liked." The "wave line theory" was carried out in her with a considerable degree of skill. In spite of the great things expected of her, however, she did not prove to be a remarkably fast boat, and in races in English waters before she came over here she gained only three first prizes and one second out of fifteen starts. Nevertheless, Mr. Ashbury challenged with her, and then the usual correspondence began. The correspondence was long and acrimonius, and at one time it seemed as if the matter would be taken to the courts. Looking back calmly on the affair at this distance of time it does not seem as if all of Mr. Ashbury's claims were entirely unreasonable, though some of them were, and he had a most aggravating manner of stating all of them. One thing which he wanted to do was to challenge in behalf of twelve yacht clubs at once, so that if he was beaten in the first race he could go on and sail eleven more, any one of which, if he won, would give him the cup. Of course in a series of twelve races it would be a poor boat indeed which would not by a "fluke" win one of them.

The New-York Yacht Club refused Mr. Ashbury's demands in this respect, but offered to accept him as the champion of the Royal Harwich Yacht Club, and sail a series of seven races against him, each with a single boat, the victory in the majority of the races to decide the possession of the cup. Finally, after threats of legal proceedings from Mr. Ashbury, and a lot of correspondence, which is of too unpleasant a nature and of too little interest at this late day to be reviewed, an understanding was reached, and the first race of the international series of 1871 was sailed on October 16, 1871. The committee of the New-York Yacht Club having the matter in charge had designated a number of schooners as a fleet from which to pick the American champion, ordering them all to be ready at the anchorage off Quarantine on the morning of the races. The regular course of the New-York Yacht Club in those days began and ended above the Narrows, off Quarantine.

In other respects it was practically as it is now. When the committee came down to the starting place on the morning of October 16 there was a light wind blowing, and the Columbia, then owned by Franklin Osgood, was selected as the champion of the club for the day. The Columbia was a light-weather boat, which the Livonia was not particularly. The Columbia had only recently been added to the fleet of the New-York Yacht Club. She registered 206 tons, as against the Livonia's 260. The following description of the Livonia is taken from The New-York Tribune of October 17, 1871:

"The distinguishing features of the schooner are that her channel pieces are filled up solid underneath, so as to afford no resistance to the water; she is provided with a jibboom instead of a bowsprit; that her jibs are all set without stays, and that her masts are placed closer together than is usually the case in the English model. Her length is 108 feet over all; length on water-line, 99 feet; breadth of beam, 23.7 feet. Her spars and rigging are of the plainest kind, and are calculated for a heavy-sea yacht. Her sails are of American cotton duck, and set to perfection."

It was against this boat that the Columbia started at 10:40 o'clock. A light but steady wind was blowing from the northwest, and a strong ebb tide was running. The yachts set all their light sails, and the Columbia felt the breeze first and took the lead, which she maintained to the finish. After passing the Southwest Spit Buoy the wind hauled to the westward and freshened a little. The Columbia sailed closer to the wind than the Livonia, and was favored in every respect with just the wind and water for her light draught. The time of the yachts at the different marks was as follows:

	S. W. Spit.	Lightship.	S. W. Spit.	Finish.
Columbia	12:04:00	1:23:53	3:50:13	4:57:42
Livonia	12:08:27	1:32:31	4:19:50	5:23:00

The time of the race was as follows:

	Elapsed time.	Corrected time.
Columbia	6:17:42	6:19:41
Livonia	6:43:00	6:46:43

The second race of the series was sailed on October 18. The race was to have been over a course twenty miles to windward and return from the Sandy Hook Lightship. After the stakeboat had been sent out for the outer mark, however, the wind, which had been blowing from the west and was expected to haul to the southwest, changed instead to blow from northnorthwest, thereby defeating the object of the committee, and giving the yachts a free wind over the entire course. The breeze had freshened considerably, and was blowing strong and steady when the yachts were started. The Columbia had again been chosen as the club's champion. The Livonia was beautifully handled and crossed the line first under mainsail, foresail, club topsail, main-topmast staysail, big jib, flying jib and balloon jib-topsail. The Columbia, carrying the same sails, was less than two minutes behind her. Soon after the start the Columbia parted her main-topmast staysail sheet, and had to take in the sail. In about ten minutes she had the sail set again. The wind continued to freshen until it was blowing half a gale. As the stakeboat

was approached the Livonia was still leading, but was to leeward, and it was evident that the Columbia had gained on her on the way out. The Livonia when near the stakeboat hauled up close on the wind, crossed the bow of the Columbia, and passed the stakeboat on the starboard hand.

The Columbia rounded the stakeboat, leaving it on the port hand, tacked and started for home. Both yachts had shortened sail now. The Livonia in attempting to gibe around the stakeboat had got in irons and lost considerable time. There was considerable sea on, but the shallow American boat steadily gained on the Livonia, and stood up much stiffer than her antagonist. The Columbia finally swept by the judges' boat about half a mile ahead of the Livonia. The time of the race was as follows:

	Start.	Finish.	Elapsed time.	Corrected time.
Columbia	12:05:36½	3:07:15	3:01:38½	3:07:41¾
Livonia	12:03:20½	3:10:10	3:06:49½	3:15:15½

The Columbia was therefore the winner. Mr Ashbury entered a protest against the victory being awarded to the Columbia in this race on the ground that the Columbia had left the stakeboat on the wrong side in rounding it. As no directions as to which side the stakeboat should be left on had been given, the committee refused to entertain the protest.

The third race of the series was sailed on October 19. It had not been the intention of the committee to again put the Columbia in, and it had been so understood by her owner and the crew. Therefore after the race of the day before no attempt had been made to get the boat ready for another contest, and officers and crew had set up late talking over the double victory of the yacht and properly celebrating it. Besides this they worked like beavers in the race and were pretty well exhausted. Something was the matter with all the other boats of the selected fleet, however, not one of them being in a fit condition to race, and the Columbia was sent out for a third time. The selection of a boat took three hours, and The Tribune's account of the race says that "everybody, except Mr. Ashbury, entirely lost his patience." The race was sailed over the club course of the New-York Yacht Club, and was won by the Livonia. The race seems to have been a bungle all around, and there is little pertaining to it upon which Americans can look back with pride. The unreadiness of the boats which should have been ready even down to the scouring of the cooks' kettles and pans upon such an occasion, the carelessness by which the Columbia was dropped to leeward of the stakeboat by the tug which towed her down to the start, and the various ways in which the Columbia went to pieces are all unpleasant to think about. The Livonia took the lead at the start and held it to the finish. When the Columbia was nearing the Southwest Spit buoy she carried away her flying jib stay. When near the same buoy coming back her steering gear carried away, and she came near drifting in the shoals. When the steering gear was repaired she carried away her main topmast staysail sheet. In short, the American boat was not in the race from start to finish. There was a good sailing breeze from west-southwest, and a smooth sea. The official time of the race was as follows:

	Start.	Finish.	Elapsed time.	Corrected time.
Livonia	1 :25 :00	5 :18 :05	3 :53 :05	4 :02 :25
Columbia	1 :25 :00	5 :37 :38	4 :12 :38	4 :17 :35

Everything considered, it is a wonder that the Columbia made such a good showing as she did in actual time. On October 23 was sailed the fourth race of the series, and this time the Sappho was matched against the Livonia. Before starting in the race Mr. Ashbury sent a note to the committee, saying "I continue the series of races without prejudice to my confirmed claim." He referred to his protest regarding the race of October 18. The race was twenty miles to windward and return from Sandy Hook Lightship. A moderate breeze was blowing, and Mr. Ashbury got just what he had been wanting—

the Southwest Spit was reached the Sappho overhauled her and took the lead. This lead she kept increasing all the time. The time of the race was as follows:

	Start.	Finish.	Elapsed time.	Corrected time.
Sappho	11 :21 :00	3 :59 :05	4 :38 :05	4 :46 :17
Livonia	11 :21 :00	4 :25 :41	5 :04 :41	5 :11 :44

The Americans having won four races out of five in the series of seven, the committee declared the series closed, and that the custody of the cup shall still remain with the New-York Yacht Club. The Livonia had been beaten twice by a centreboard boat, the Columbia, and twice by a keel boat, the Sappho. Mr. Ashbury, however, was not satisfied. He still claimed the race of October 18, and having announced to the committee that he would send his boat out to Sandy Hook lightship on a certain day, he did go there, and raced with the Dauntless. The club, however,

THE SAPPHO ROUNDING THE LIGHTSHIP.

a dead beat to windward. The Sappho proved herself better both on the wind and off the wind than the Livonia, and kept increasing her lead from start to finish. The official time of the race was as follows:

	Start.	Finish.	Elapsed time.	Corrected time.
Sappho	12 :11 :00	5 :44 :24	5 :33 :24	5 :36 :02
Livonia	12 :12 :52	6 :17 :30	6 :04 :38	6 :09 :23

The fifth and last race of the series for the cup was sailed over the New-York Yacht Club course on October 23. The Sappho was again the chosen champion of the Americans, and again she won. There was a moderate breeze blowing from west-southwest and the tide was the last of the ebb at the start. It was a clear and beautiful day of Indian summer, and a great flotilla of yachts and excursion steamers came out to see the race. The Livonia crossed the line first and started down the bay at a good pace, but before

took no cognizance of this race, and not much of Mr. Ashbury. Mr. Ashbury now claimed the cup, and there was some correspondence of a rather bitter nature. He had presented to the New-York Yacht Club two challenge cups. The club returned the cups to Mr. Ashbury, not feeling it the proper thing to retain them under the circumstances. Among other things, Mr. Ashbury directly accused the club of "sharp practice." It was a relief to everybody when he went home to England. His demands were declared unreasonable and his manner of making them was condemned by English as well as American yachtsmen. The departure of Mr. Ashbury closed the most unpleasant chapter in the history of the America's Cup. It is not at all probable that another one of the kind will ever have to be written.

CANADA SENT A BOAT.

THE THIRD CHALLENGE FOR THE AMERICA'S CUP.

FAILURE OF THE SCHOONER YACHT COUNTESS OF DUFFERIN TO WIN THE BLUE RIBBON OF THE SEA—WORK OF THE MADELEINE.

Early in 1876, the Centennial year, the third challenge for the America's Cup since it had been won by the America was received. It was the first one to be received from a country other than England, coming from the Royal Canadian Yacht Club in behalf of Charles Gifford, vice-commodore of the club and part owner of the schooner yacht Countess of Dufferin. Although the New-York Yacht Club had been anticipating a challenge, one was not expected from Canada, as yacht building in that country had not advanced to the point where the Canadians would be justified in hoping to carry away the cup. It seems that · P. McGiehan, a yacht designer of Pamrapo, had built for a Canadian yachtsman a sloop yacht named Cora. The Cora went to Canada and beat everything of her size there. Alexander Cuthbert, a Canadian designer of local repute, built the sloop Annie Cuthbert, which beat the Cora. Now the Cora had been considered a wonderful boat in Canada, and the yachtsmen of the Dominion did not doubt for a minute that she represented the best efforts of American yacht designing. When the Annie Cuthbert beat her the Canadians concluded that they had in Alexander Cuthbert a designer who was to astonish the world, and visions of accomplishing what the mother country had been unable to achieve, and of wresting the cup from the possession of the Americans, at once began to fill the minds of the yachtsmen of the Dominion.

Captain Cuthbert went to work on the model of a schooner which, when completed, he declared to be the finest he ever made in his life, and a syndicate was formed to. build her and send her hunting for the America's Cup. After some delay on account of lack of funds the yacht was built and named the Countess of Dufferin. When she had her trial trip in May the newspapers of the Dominion were enthusiastic over her, and declared her a marvel of speed and beauty.

Meantime the usual preliminary correspondence had been gone through with, the New-York Yacht Club cheerfully granting everything which Commodore Gifford asked regarding the terms of the race. The club named as its champion the schooner yacht Madeleine. July 10, 12 and 14 were selected as the dates of the races. These dates were subsequently changed by agreement to August 11, 12 and 14. After many delays the Canadian yacht finally arrived in New-York Harbor on July 18.

The descriptions of the two champions which were to compete for the cup were as follows: The Countess of Dufferin was 107 feet over all, 24 feet beam, and of a shallow type, drawing only 6 1-2 feet of water. Her mainmast was 65 feet and her main-topmast 30 feet long.

She had a mainboom 55 feet long, and spread 4,000 yards of canvas. She looked exactly like an American yacht, and it was evident that in modelling her Captain Cuthbert had felt the influence of the American designs which he had seen on the lakes. The Countess of Dufferin is still in existence, and is now called the Countess. She belongs to the Countess Yacht Club, of Chicago.

The Madeleine was built as a sloop by David Kirby in 1868. She was altered in 1871, '73

COUNTESS SETTING BALLOON JIB.

and '75, until there was little of the original boat left and she was a fast schooner, 107 feet over all, 95 feet on the water-line, 24 feet beam and 8 feet draught. She was always a good boat whether as sloop or schooner, but it was not until her alterations in 1873 that she took rank in the first class of fast schooners. When the Countess of Dufferin came to meet her in 1876 the Madeleine had a long record of brilliant victories behind her and she crowned her career by her brilliant defence of the cup. In 1875 the Madeleine was purchased by John S. Dickerson, her present owner.

The first time that the Countess of Dufferin had a chance to show her speed against the American yachts was in a race which she sailed for the Brenton's Reef Cup, starting on July 26. The course was from Sandy Hook lightship around Brenton's Reef lightship and return. The schooners Idler, America, Wanderer, · Tidal Wave and Countess of Dufferin started in this race. There was a fine whole-sail breeze blowing from south-southeast at the start and the Countess made a fairly good showing up to the turning of the Brenton's Reef lightship off Newport. She never had a chance of winning the race, however, and after the lightship was rounded she was practically out of the race and struggled no more. No one who saw her in this race believed that the cup was in danger.

Commodore Gifford had started out in the race with a full confidence that he would win, and even after his crushing defeat seemed to think that all he needed was a full set of "balloon" sails to beat the American yachts. The Canadians seemed to be singularly blind to the defects of their schooner, and even after the races for the cup had been sailed and the true position of the yacht as a racer settled beyond a shadow of doubt, Captain Cuthbert maintained that only a few alterations were necessary to make the Countess the fastest schooner of her size afloat.

There were few better judges of a yacht than Captain Roland Coffin and, in his "History of the America's Cup," he says of the Canadian yacht, "She was a fair model forward, but her counters were too heavy and her greatest beam was too far abaft her longitudinal centre. Then she was rough as compared with American yachts and meanly rigged and canvased. To add to these disadvantages may be added an inefficient crew."

The Countess of Dufferin having received a new foresail and a set of "balloons," she started against the Madeleine in her first race for the cup on August 11. The course was the old New-York Yacht Club course, with the start and finish off Stapleton, S. I. The Canadian yacht allowed the Madeleine one minute one second time, according to the time allowance of the New-York Yacht Club, then in vogue. This was the first race for the America's Cup where a single champion, named in advance as a representative yacht, had competed on each side. When the cup of the Royal Yacht Squadron was first won by the America, international yacht racing was in its incipiency. The conditions of a sport as far reaching and as important could not be struck out--as "Jo" Gargery struck out his father's epitaph—at one blow. It had to be a process of evolution and of the experiences which come with it before the yachting world could arrive at the point when it was sure that the best and fairest way for two nations to contend against each other for the sovereignty of the yachting seas was to choose champions, go out and do battle as warriors of old decided battles on the gage of single combat between the lines of watching armies.

At the first race between the Countess of Dufferin and the Madeleine there was a great outpouring of yachts and excursion steamers. The public did not understand the significance of the Brenton's Reef race, and there was more or less anxiety as to the outcome of the race, and there was a great curiosity to see the sailing of the much-vaunted Canadian champion. The tide was at the last quarter of the flood when the starting signal was given to the yachts at 11:05 a. m. The Canadian yacht had an opportunity to start first, as she was in a better position, a sloop having forced the Madeleine about, but she bore up before reaching the line, and the Madeleine went over first. There was not much difference between them at the start—less than a minute—but the Madeleine went over under good headway, and blanketed the Countess just before she did so. The wind drew up through the Narrows so that the yachts had work dead to windward to do before they got through between the bluffs, and were out in the broad waters of the Lower Bay. The Countess went to the west bank when the yachts had got through the Narrows, and the Madeleine went hunting for wind over in Gravesend Bay. Outside the wind was blowing a good sailing breeze from the south-

southeast, and the water was smooth. The yachts worked their way down to the Southwest Spit, the Madeleine gaining all the time and opening a space between herself and the Countess of Dufferin. After the first search for wind and tides over in Gravesend Bay the Madeleine had come back to her antagonist and never after that did she go off looking for more favorable conditions, but kept in the same wind and water. The times of rounding the Southwest Spit buoy were as follows:

Madeleine 1:19:19
Countess of Dufferin...................................1:26:32

A strong ebb tide was now running, and the yachts made good time out by the point of the Hook. The Madeleine overstood the mark boat off the point of the Hook and lost about five minutes by so doing. The Countess crawled up on her, and through the American champion went for the lightship at a rattling pace with sheets free, her antagonist was not so far behind her when the outer mark was rounded.

After rounding the lightship the Madeleine ran up her balloon jib-topsail and maintopmast staysail in forty-eight seconds. The Countess took fully three minutes to do the same thing. Then the Madeleine began to run away from the Countess, and, as if tired of "fooling," sped on by the Hook, passing into the main ship channel seven minutes ahead of the Canadian yacht. At the Southwest Spit on the return the time of the yachts was as follows:

Madeleine 3:57:28
Countess of Dufferin...................................4:06:48

The Madeleine then sprang up the Bay and arrived at the finish an easy winner. The gain made by the Madeleine in the run up from the Southwest Spit is not shown by the table, as the finish in those days was off Stapleton, and as soon as a yacht got inside the Narrows she naturally lost the wind and went slowly to the finish, while the boat outside was going fast with the full force of the breeze. The following is the table of the time of the race:

	Start.	Finish.	Elapsed time.	Corrected time.
Madeleine	11:16:31	4:41:26	5:24:55	5:23:54
Countess of Dufferin	11:17:03	4:51:50	5:34:53	5:34:53

The Tribune of August 12, 1876, said in its account of the race: "The yachts were at no time during the race close enough together to admit of any 'jockeying,' even if it were desired by either party. The Madeleine took the lead and held it throughout, arriving at her anchorage and having all sails furled before the Countess was opposite the clubhouse."

The second and closing race of the series was over a course twenty miles to sea, from the point of the Hook and return. The course was to be twenty miles to windward and return, but the perverseness of the wind made it a reach out and

run back. In this race the America accompanied the yachts over the course, and proved that, as old as she was, she was a better boat than the Countess. It was shortly after noon when the yachts were started. The Madeleine went over first, followed in a few seconds by the Countess. The Countess would not sail so close to the wind as the Madeleine, and when her sailing master "pinched" her she dropped so far astern that he gave her a good fill, and finally got abeam of the Madeleine, but far and away to leeward. So when the two yachts came to round the outer mark the case of the Canadian champion was most hopeless. The wind was light and the sea smooth in this race, and the time was as follows:

	Start.	Finish.	Elapsed time.	Corrected time.
Madeleine	12:17:24	7:37:11	7:19:47	7:18:46
Countess of Dufferin	12:17:58	8:03:58	7:46:00	7:46:00

This settled the matter of the possession of the cup for that year, and the Countess of Dufferin was laid up in a basin at Staten Island. Then began financial complications and legal processes between her owners, and the next year she was sold at Sheriff's sale and taken over to South Brooklyn. From there she was taken to New-York waters. There were several claims against the yacht, and finally she was quietly taken away to Canada. The ambition of the Canadians had come to naught, and the yacht which had come for the great cup heralded with trumpets and the clanging of sounding brass went back in disgrace and defeat.

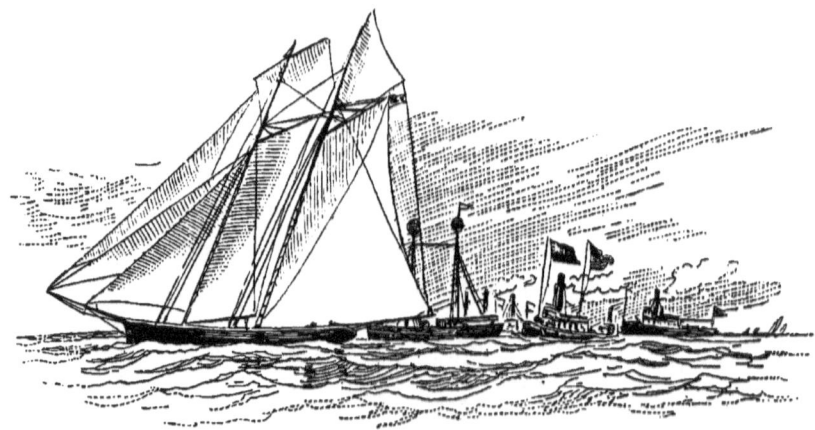

MADELEINE PASSING THE LIGHTSHIP.

CANADA FAILED AGAIN.

HER SECOND FUTILE ATTEMPT TO WIN THE AMERICA'S CUP.

ATALANTA NOT ONLY WAS SLOW BUT SHE WAS POORLY HANDLED—RACES WHICH WERE NOT RACES.

The fifth race for the America's Cup, counting as one the race in which the America won the trophy, was of little value of itself and proved nothing except that the Canadians had not kept pace with the Americans in yacht building or yacht sailing. Four years had elapsed since, in 1876, the Canadians had made their futile attempt to capture the cup with the Countess of Dufferin, when the Atalanta came here as champion of the Bay of Quinte Yacht Club to try for the cup. If she was a fair specimen of a Canadian yacht, and she was presumed to be, she showed no advancement at all over the Countess, and was so badly handled that the races were almost farcical. Since the Cambria and Livonia races, yacht building had advanced rapidly in England, and there were many boats on the other side which could easily have defeated the sloops which "made a show" of the Canadian Atalanta, for yacht building in this country had not

THE ATALANTA.

made progress as it had in England. But this the English were not sure of, and the Americans did not believe. There had been no races between representative yachts of England and America since the Livonia came over, and so the two nations had no means of gauging the progress

of each other. The Americans believed the Gracie, Fanny, Mischief and Arrow to be the fastest sloops in the world, and they had every reason so to believe. Compared to the Atalanta any one of these boats was as a winged-heeled Mercury to a tortoise. In the same year that the Atalanta came, however, there came another boat, a little cutter from England called the Madge. Before the international races were sailed the little cutter sailed a series of races with American sloops of her size, and she was a revelation. To all those who had eyes not blinded by prejudice she showed exactly how Americans stood in yacht building compared with England, how they had stagnated and what would have been the result if, instead of being a little boat sent over on the deck of a steamer, she had been a big cutter with a challenge for the cup. She was a positive shock to the complacency of American yachtsmen, and while the victory over the Atalanta added nothing to American yachting except the prestige of another victory, the cutter Madge set going that great revival of continued progress in American yacht building which was later illuminated by the genius of Burgess, and which for rapidity of development and brilliancy of successful achievement has exceeded anything the world has ever seen. It soon brought America ahead of England and inspired that close, keen rivalry between the two countries in the matter of yacht building which has been so beneficial to both.

It should be said that the Madge was a Scottish boat, designed by Watson. Nominally, however, the contest between the Mischief and Atalanta was, of course, the chief yachting incident of the year.

It was early in 1881 that news reached New-York that Captain Cuthbert, the designer of the Countess of Dufferin, was building a big sloop, and, undismayed by his previous failure, was going to challenge for the America's Cup. He had joined the Bay of Quinte Yacht Club, of Belleville, Ont., and that club was to be the one to challenge for the cup. On May 16 the Bay of Quinte Yacht Club sent its formal challenge on behalf of Captain Cuthbert to the New-York Yacht Club. The Atalanta was named as the Canadian champion, and it was asked that the six months' notice required by the deed of gift be waived, as it could be, according to the terms of the deed, at the option of the club holding the trophy. The New-York Yacht Club at once held a special meeting, accepted the challenge, proposed that a series of three races be sailed and appointed a special committee to arrange the details.

The Bay of Quinte Yacht Club demanded that the New-York Yacht Club name one yacht, which should sail in all three races. To this the New-York Yacht Club readily consented. In fact, the club conceded everything which Captain Cuthbert wished. As soon as it was settled that there was to be a race for the cup, the New-York Yacht Club's committee went about the work of selecting a boat. The sloop Arrow, built by David Kirby, of Rye, Westchester, had the best record for speed at that time. She was owned by Ross Winans, of Philadelphia. Mr.

Winans was not a member of the club, nor was he in the country, so it was determined to telegraph to him, offering to buy the boat. Mr. Kirby, however, told the flag officers of the club that as he was the designer of the Arrow he knew her defects, and was confident that he could build a faster boat. The flag officers of the club at that time were John R. Waller, commodore; James D. Smith, vice-commodore, and Hermann Oelrichs, rear commodore. They gave Mr. Kirby an order to build a yacht, and he produced the Pocahontas. She was said at the time to be an enlarged Arrow, and Mr. Kirby was confident that in her he had improved on the Arrow. The Gracie, owned by Charles R. Flint and Joseph P. Earle; the Mischief, owned by J. R. Busk; the Hildegard, owned by Hermann Oelrichs, and the Pocahontas, owned by

She had proved herself in every way unworthy of the high hopes entertained of her. The Mischief and Gracie made a fine race of it, and the Mischief won by 14 seconds. The Mischief was therefore chosen as the American champion. The Gracie was a more popular boat than the Mischief, and many wished that the choice had fallen upon her. There was a sharp rivalry between the two yachts and their speed was so nearly equal that the New-York yachtsmen of those days were divided into two hostile camps, the partisans of the Gracie and the partisans of the Mischief. Therefore the special committee kept which boat they had selected a dark secret until the morning of the day fixed for the first international race, November 8.

The Canadian yacht arrived here on October 30. She came through the Oswego and Erie

Atalanta.   Mischief.

THE START FOR THE CUP.
(By permission of Charles Scribner's Sons.)

the flag officers of the club, were chosen to sail in trial races for the purpose of selecting a winner. The yachts started over the New-York Yacht Club course in the first of the trial races on October 13. Before getting through the Narrows a strong puff of wind came over the Staten Island hills, and the topmasts of the Gracie and Pocahontas went by the board. The race was won by the Mischief. On October 19 the second trial race was sailed, only the Gracie, Pocahontas and Mischief starting. The Gracie won, beating the Mischief by three minutes and nineteen seconds. The Pocahontas proved that she was a flat failure, and was far behind at the finish.

The third trial race was sailed over a course outside the Hook on October 20. Mischief, Gracie and Pocahontas were the competitors. The Pocahontas was so badly disabled that she was towed back to a sheltering basin and laid up.

canals, for she was, like the Countess of Dufferin, a fresh-water yacht, built on Lake Ontario. She came through the "raging canawl" in safety, which, in view of her subsequent performances, unkind critics declared, was remarkable. She was put in drydock at once and work was pushed forward on her to get her ready for the race. It had been originally asked by the Canadians that the races for the cup be sailed in September, but owing to delay in launching the Atalanta a postponement had been asked for and granted. When the Atalanta was placed in drydock the practised eye at once saw that there was nothing new or startling in her lines and no indication of great speed. Still, though her model was sharply criticised, opinions concerning her were not all unfavorable. Finally the Atalanta was ready. The day named for the first race was foggy, and there was so little wind that it was determined to postpone it until the next day, November 9. On that day the Mischief and Atalanta were started in the first race over the old New-York Yacht Club course, the start being off Stapleton. The Gracie was on hand at the start and went over the course with the other two yachts, beating both the Atalanta and Mischief to the consequent glorification of her many partisans. In fact, about all the racing there was after Southwest Spit buoy was reached was between the two American sloops, the Atalanta being out of the race before she reached the first mark.

The wind at the start was blowing a good sailing breeze from west-southwest, and the tide was the last of the flood. At 11:11 the starting signal was given and the yachts crossed on the starboard tack. The Mischief led the Atalanta over the line by one minute one second. Neither yacht had her topsail set, and the Atalanta had a reef in her mainsail. In the lower bay both yachts set their working topsails. The Mischief constantly drawing away from the Atalanta the latter boat shook out her reef, but as her topsail was set flying she had to take in that sail for a while in order that the halyards might be bent lower on the sprit. The crew of the Atalanta was composed largely of volunteers from the Bay of Quinte Yacht Club, and there seemed nothing like discipline or quick, sharp work on board the Canadian. The times of the races at the Southwest Spit buoy were as follows:

Mischief 12:33:12
Atalanta 12:45:27

From here out to the Sandy Hook lightship the Atalanta was so far astern as to deprive the contest between her and the Mischief of any interest. Try as she might the Canadian boat could not close up the great gap between her and the Mischief. That she was not well sailed is admitted, but had she been sailed by the best yachting talent the world ever saw she never, from start to finish would have had a ghost of a show of winning the race. The spectators who had come out in tugs and yachts and steamers to see the race ceased to take any thing except a languid interest in the Atalanta and devoted themselves to looking at the fine work being done by the Gracie. The times of the Atalanta and Mischief at the lightship were as follows:

Mischief 1:25:25
Atalanta 1:38:14

On the run in the yachts had a cracking breeze, and at the Southwest Spit the Atalanta was too far astern to be timed. The time of the race was as follows:

Name.	Start.	Finish	Elapsed Time.	Corrected Time.
Mischief	11:14:50	3:31:59	4:17:09	4:17:09
Atalanta	11:15:51	4:04:15¼	4:48:24¼	4:45:29¼

The Mischief beat the Atalanta 28 minutes 20 1-4 seconds on corrected time, and 31 minutes 15 1-4 seconds on actual time.

The second race of the series was sailed on November 10. The result being a foregone conclusion little interest was taken in the contest. It seemed almost cruel to race against such a boat as the Atalanta had proved herself to be. There

was no sport in it, only expense and trouble, and all wished it were well over with. The second race was started off the point of the Hook, and the course was twenty miles to leeward and return in the open ocean. The wind blew a fresh whole-sail breeze from west by north. The boats ran for the outer mark with booms to port and jib-topsails "whiskered out" to starboard. They carried club-topsails. The Mischief crossed the starting line twenty seconds ahead of the Atalanta. The Canadian boat did better in the run out than she had ever done before, and held the Mischief well. Both boats took in their topsails and reefed their mainsails as the outer mark was approached. The times at the outer mark were as follows:

Mischief 1:40:14
Atalanta 1:42:29½

Now it came to windward work, and it was "all day" with the Atalanta. The Mischief constantly drew away from her, gaining on every tack, and at the finish had beaten her worse than she did on the previous day. The Atalanta had to put a second reef in her mainsail on the way in. The time of the race was as follows:

Name.	Start.	Finish.	Elapsed Time.	Corrected Time.
Mischief	11:58:17	4:53:10	4:54:53	4:54:53
Atalanta	11:58:47	5:35:19	5:36:32	5:33:47

Thus the Mischief beat the Atalanta 38 minutes 54 seconds on corrected time, and 41 minutes 39 seconds on actual time. Even this most crushing defeat did not make Captain Cuthbert lose confidence in himself or his boat, and he at once announced that he would lay the Atalanta up for the winter and challenge again, when, with his boat in better condition, he should expect a more favorable result. He never did challenge again, however.

The Atalanta was a centreboard sloop 70 feet over all, 64 feet on the water line, 19 feet beam, 6 feet 10 inches depth of hold, and 5 feet 6 inches draught aft and 3 feet 6 inches forward. With her board down she drew 16 feet 6 inches. She had a 70-foot lower-mast and a 34-foot topmast. She had 25 feet of bowsprit outboard, a 70-foot boom, and a 36-foot gaff. The Mischief, which defeated her, an iron centreboard sloop, was designed by A. Cary Smith, and built by Harlan & Hollingsworth in 1879. She is now owned by Edward F. Linton, of New-York.

The defence of the America's Cup is a rather expensive operation. These farcical races with the Atalanta cost the New-York Yacht Club over $20,000, and it was felt that something ought to be done to protect the club against such attempts as that of the Atalanta. The result was the returning of the cup to the only survivor of the original givers—George L. Schuyler—who gave it back to the club under a new deed of gift. Thus the challenge of the Atalanta was unfortunate in every way, for it not only brought about foolish races for a trophy for which only the best yachts of the world are expected to contend, and caused great expense and annoyance, with no results of value whatever, but it also ultimately brought about the second deed of gift—a precedent for the third deed of gift, and international and domestic discussions over these instruments have not yet ceased. It was not until December, 1882, that the New-York Yacht Club decided to give the cup back to Mr. Schuyler. The second deed of gift was as follows:

" Any organized yacht club of any foreign country, incorporated, patented or licensed by the legislature, admiralty or other executive department, having for its annual regatta an ocean water-course on the sea or an arm of the sea (or one which combines both), practicable for vessels of 300 tons, shall always be entitled, through one or more of its members, to the right of sailing a match for this cup with a yacht or other vessel propelled by sails only, and constructed in the country to which the challenging club belongs, against any one yacht or vessel, as aforesaid, constructed in the country of the club holding the cup. The yacht or vessel to be of not less than thirty nor more than 300 tons, measured by the Custom House rule in use by the country of the challenging party. The challenging party shall give six months' notice in writing, naming the day of the proposed race, which day shall not be less than seven months from the day of the notice.

" The parties intending to sail for the cup may, by mutual consent, make any arrangement satisfactory to both as to the date, course, time, time allowance, number of trials, rules and sailing regulations, and any and all other conditions of the match, in which case, also, the six months' notice may be waived.

" In case the parties cannot mutually agree upon the terms of a match, then the challenging party shall have the right to contest for the cup in one trial sailed over the usual course of the annual regatta of the club holding the cup, subject to its rules and sailing regulations, the challenged party not being required to name its representative until the time agreed upon for the start.

" Accompanying the six months' notice there must be a Custom House certificate of the measurement, and a statement of the dimensions, rig and name of the vessel. No vessel which has once been defeated in a contest for this cup can be again selected by any club for its representative until after a contest for it by some other vessel has intervened, or until after the expiration of two years from the time such contest has taken place.

" Vessels intending to compete for this cup must proceed under sail on their own bottoms to the port where the contest is to take place. Should the club holding the cup be for any cause dissolved, the cup shall be handed over to any club of the same nationality it may select, which comes under the foregoing rules.

" It is to be distinctly understood that the cup is to be the property of the club, and not of the owners of the vessel winning it in a match, and that the condition of keeping it open to be sailed for by organized yacht clubs of all foreign countries upon the terms above laid down, shall forever attach to it, thus making it perpetually a challenge cup for friendly competition between foreign countries."

THE RACE OF RACES.

HOW THE GENESTA NOBLY CONTENDED FOR THE AMERICA'S CUP.

A GALLANT YACHTSMAN OWNED HER, AND IN
HIS DEFEAT THERE WAS NO SHAME—THE
PURITAN'S MAGNIFICENT WORK.

It was early in 1885 that the New-York Yacht Club received a challenge for the America's Cup from the Royal Yacht Squadron. It was the Royal Yacht Squadron which first offered the cup, and this was the first time it had challenged for it since it had been won by the America. The cutter Genesta was named as the boat to compete. She was owned by Sir Richard Sutton, a young baronet well known in England as a thorough yachtsman and sportsman of the highest type, and who subsequently won the admiration of all Americans for the gentlemanly and true sportsmanlike qualities which he showed in

GENESTA.

his contest for the cup. It was at first proposed that if the Genesta failed to win the cup the Galatea, a cutter belonging to Lieutenant Henn, of the Royal Navy, and a member of the Royal Northern Yacht Club, should race for the trophy after a brief time. There was the usual amount of correspondence and all that sort of thing, but finally it was so arranged that the Genesta raced for the cup in the fall of 1885 and the Galatea came over and raced for it the next year.

The contest for the cup that year brought to public view the genius of Burgess and broke down the prejudice which had been hampering the development of American yachting. The **races** of the Genesta and Puritan began that rapid

interchange of ideas between the two nations of England and America which has brought about the present condition of affairs and made the terms of cutter and sloop to lose their meaning of signifying radically opposed types. The Genesta came the nearest to taking back the cup to England of any boat before or since which has come over for it. Lord Dunraven, the present challenger for the cup, says of the Genesta: "The Genesta was a first-class vessel; if not the best, she was at least the second best English yacht of her size afloat at the time, and she made a creditable fight."

In the light of the Genesta's performances on the other side there seems little doubt that she was the best all-around boat of her size on the other side at the time, and could fairly be considered as representing the best of British skill in yacht designing. She was designed by J. Beavor Webb, now of this city. As soon as it was settled that there was to be a race for the cup the New-York Yacht Club sent out a circular to all the yacht clubs of the United States inviting them to furnish a boat to be entered in the trial races to select a champion. The flag officers of the New-York Yacht Club, James Gordon Bennett and William P. Douglas, gave A. Cary Smith an order to design a centreboard sloop of about the length of the Genesta, and some gentlemen of the Eastern Yacht Club formed a syndicate and ordered a cup defender from Edward Burgess. The principal members of the Eastern syndicate were General Charles J. Paine and J. Malcolm Forbes.

Burgess had a local reputation as a yacht designer, but was not well known outside of Massachusetts. He had taken up yacht designing as a hobby in the days of his wealth, and when financial reverses compelled him to work for his daily bread he had gone into it as a business. He had been successful in designing small boats, and General Paine and Mr. Forbes had confidence in him. A. Cary Smith was then, and is now, one of the best and the best-known designers of the country, a man who never built a bad boat, and it was to the boat designed by him that most people looked as the yacht to save the cup, although there was a general doubt if faster sloops could be built than the Mischief and Gracie. This doubt, it may be said, however, was not strong in the minds of well-informed yachtsmen who knew what wonderful strides yacht building had made on the other side, and had heeded the lessons taught by the cutter Madge. In fact, there was a strong party of the most progressive yachtsmen who did not believe it possible in the condition of American yachting at that time to build a boat on this side to beat the English champion. The Priscilla was built by the Harlan & Hollingsworth Company at Wilmington, Del. She was of iron and of the following dimensions: Length over all 94 feet, on water-line 85 feet, beam 22 feet 5 inches, draught 7 feet 9 inches. The Puritan was built at Lawley's yard at Boston. She was 93 feet over all, 80 feet on the water-line, 23 feet beam, and drew 8 feet 2 inches of water. She was built of wood and was, like the Priscilla, a centreboard. Both boats are

still in existence, the Priscilla as the schooner
Elma, and the Puritan under her old form and
name.

Tho Genesta, built on the Clyde, was launched
in May of 1884. She was of composite build, that
is, with a steel frame and elm and teak plank-
ing. She was 90 feet over all, 81 feet on the
water line, 15 feet beam and 13 feet 6 inches
draught.   Sho arrived in New-York on July
16, 1885, having made the extremely fast time
for a boat of her size across the Atlantic of twenty-
four days, and doing it under a jury rig.   Her
record on the other side was well known, and
yachtsmen felt a little nervous about her.   When
she got her racing spars in and went sailing about
tho bay to get "tuned up" she displayed qualities
which far from allayed this anxiety.   Every day
she went sailing about in the Lower Bay, towing
a little pumpkin seed boat astern, and yachts
used to run out and try to get a brush with her, so
as to take her measure.   But the Genesta was
wary, and avoided all offers of battle.   Anxious
watchers, among whom was the writer, who used
to observe her daily from the heights of Fort
Wadsworth, saw enough of what she could do,
however, to disturb their peace of mind.   The
Genesta's quickness in stays was one thing which
especially struck that little group of yachting
critics, and the writer remembers several learned
dissertations in   which it was sought to be
demonstrated that this was a positive disadvantage.

Well, the Puritan arrived from Boston, and
came in for a good share of criticism, and   the
Priscilla came up from Wilmington, and came in
for a good share of praise, and the old
guard sneered at both of them and declared that
Mischief and Gracie could beat them both with
time allowance.

On August 21 the first of the trial races was
sailed, and Burgess and the Puritan burst upon
the yachting world.   The race was in charge of
a special committee appointed by the New-York
Yacht Club, consisting of J. Frederick Tams,
Philip Schuyler, C. H. Stebbins, Jules A. Montant
and J. R. Busk.   The course was twenty miles to
windward, from the Scotland Light Ship and return.   The yachts starting in the race were the
Puritan, Priscilla, Gracie and Bedouin.   The
Bedouin is a cutter of the beamy type.   The
Tribune said of the race next day:

"The Yankee sloop Puritan, over forty miles of
rough water in a stiff breeze yesterday, not only
demonstrated that she was the fastest sloop ever
launched on this side the water, but gave promise
that the cup which seemed to be slipping from the
country's grasp would be retained for some time
longer in the 'land of the free and the home of the
brave.'   The performance of the Puritan was the
most wonderful ever seen in these waters.   Her
speed was phenomenal, her sailing superb and she
herself seemed perfect.   The renowned Gracie, the
ambitious Priscilla and the swift Bedouin were
left so far behind that the race was decided before
it was well begun.   The white sloop from Boston
out-footed and out-pointed everything.   She beat
the Priscilla 11 minutes 12 seconds, the Bedouin
18 minutes 46 seconds and the Gracie 35 minutes
53 seconds."

The second of the trial races was sailed on
August 22 over a triangular course in the open sea.
The wind was light and did not hold steady.   The
Puritan had the race, when the wind shifted and
brought the Priscilla in a winner by a "fluke."
The same four yachts started then as in the first
race.   The victory of the Priscilla was a barren
one, only achieved by an accident, and did not
make her even a formidable rival to Puritan.
The first day's race was a fair test, and nothing
could take away its glory from the Puritan.

The third of the trial races was sailed over the
New-York Yacht Club course and resulted in a
victory for the Puritan.   Thereupon the committee selected that boat as the American champion,
though the formal announcement was not made
until September 1.   By the terms of agreement
with Sir Richard Sutton, the club had agreed to
name its champion one week before the first race
for the cup.   The dates for the races for the cup
were fixed as September 7, 9 and 11.

Now, all American yachtsmen were delighted
with the Puritan, and an easy victory over the
Genesta was looked forward to.   The first race
was to be twenty miles to windward and return
from Scotland Lightship, and on the morning of
September 8 the Puritan and Genesta went out to
the starting place accompanied by an enormous
flotilla of all sorts of craft which the great port
of New-York could furnish.   The yachts were
started, but the winds were variable and so light
that the attempt to get over the course was given
up after about five hours of little more than drifting, and the yachts were towed back to harbor.
The Puritan in the work of the day, unsatisfactory
as it was, had shown such good qualities that her
admirers, and they were the entire population of
these United States, were more enthusiastic than
ever about her, and confident of the result of the
races.

A second fruitless attempt to sail a race was
made the next day—September 8.   It resulted in
the Puritan and Genesta fouling each other,
the tearing of the American's boat mainsail
and the loss of the English boat's bowsprit.   The
collision occurred just as the yachts were coming up to the line for the start and were
manoeuvring for position.   It was the Puritan's
fault, and as the preparatory signal had been
given the yachts were technically in the race.
Therefore the Puritan was disqualified, and Sir
Richard Sutton was told that he could sail
over the course and claim the race.

This Sir Richard absolutely refused to do,
saying he "wanted a race and not a walkover."
This refusal of Sir Richard to take the
race, which he had every technical right to take, at
once made him a most popular man throughout
the country.   It was only a sample of the spirit
shown by the owner of the Genesta in all the
intercourse between himself and American yachtsmen while he was in this country.

On the morning of September 11 the Puritan
and Genesta, having been repaired, went out to
Scotland Lightship to make another attempt to
sail a race for the cup.   In the morning there
was every prospect of a good race, but the wind
began to drop soon after the yachts started, and
they were unable to make the course in the

prescribed time limit of seven hours. There was a heavy sea all day, and the yachts worked through it as best they could in the constantly failing wind until about sunset, when the judges' boat signalled that the race was off and the yachts were turned back before they had reached the outer mark.

In the day's work the Puritan apparently had the advantage of the Genesta, taking the seas more easily. The next day another futile attempt to sail a race was made. This time course, and the Puritan gave the Genesta an allowance of twenty-eight seconds over it according to the rules of the New-York Yacht Club, under which the boats sailed. The wind at the start was blowing lightly from the southwest, and a strong flood tide was running. The wind drew up through the Narrows so that at the starting line it was more southerly than it was outside. Aubury Crocker was sailing-master of the Puritan, and Captain Carter, the same who is now sailing-master of the Valkyrie, was at the helm

THE PURITAN CROSSING THE LINE.

the yachts were becalmed at the start, and after a weary wait for wind were turned back to harbor. It did seem as if there never was to be a real race, and the public had got tired of getting up early in the morning to go outside Sandy Hook and see "fizzles," but they were all out again the next day.

On Monday, however, there really was a race. That day had been set for the race over the New-York Yacht Club course, and the race over the outside course had been by mutual consent postponed until Tuesday. The New-York Yacht Club then had its starting place off Stapleton, and its finish below the Narrows. It was a 38-mile of the Genesta. The yachts were started at 10:30 o'clock. They went over the line side by side on the starboard tack, the Puritan being timed two seconds ahead of the Genesta only. They made two tacks above the Narrows, and then a long leg, standing well down beyond Coney Island Point. When well out in the Lower Bay the wind died out, and the Puritan hung becalmed off the West Bank. She had got a good lead on the Genesta, but now the English yacht crawled up on her until she, too, struck the glassy streak in the water where the Puritan lay and hung motionless on the tide. Then a wind came freshening up from the south, and the yachts were in motion again. They went tacking down to the Southwest Spit Buoy, the Puritan, which had got the wind first, constantly increasing her lead. When the yachts got outside the Hook there was a good stiff breeze blowing, and a heavy swell rolled up from the south.

The Puritan lead the Genesta nearly five minutes around the lightship. When the yachts came back and got in the Lower Bay they lost the wind for a while, but finally got enough to carry them home in good style. The Puritan led from the start to finish and beat the Genesta 16 minutes 47 seconds on actual time, and 16 minutes 19 seconds on corrected time. The time of the race was as follows:

Name.	Start. h. m. s.	Finish. h. m. s.	Elapsed time. h. m. s.	Corrected time. h. m. s.
Puritan	10:32:00	4:38:05	0:06:05	0:06:05
Genesta	10:32:00	4:54:52	6:22:52	0:22:24

The starting time of both yachts was taken as 10:32.00, the starting signal having been given at 10:30 o'clock and only two minutes having been allowed to cross the line. Thus the Puritan was handicapped 2 seconds and the Genesta 4 seconds.

There was naturally much rejoicing over the victory of the Puritan, but the friends of the Genesta were not discouraged, and said: "Wait until the races on the open sea." As a matter of fact, while the victory of the Puritan was encouraging, it was no guarantee of what would happen in a race outside, the New-York Yacht Club course being no place for a decisive test of the qualities of a big boat. The Genesta cracked her masthead in the race of Monday, so Wednesday was set for the first outside race.

The race of Wednesday was over the course of twenty miles to leeward and return, from the Scotland Lightship. There was a stiff breeze blowing and a lumpy sea. The Puritan saved the day and the cup by 1 minute 38 seconds. The yachts were started at 11:05. The yachts came over the line with a rush, the Genesta leading by a little over half a minute. They both set spinnakers, and the Puritan had up a big jib-topsail. Both yachts were towering piles of canvas, and never before in these waters if, indeed, anywhere in the world, had yachts sailed so fast before. Slowly but surely the Yankee boat drew up on the Genesta, and when off Sandy Hook Lightship she got so close astern as to take the British boat's wind and then shot ahead of her, going to the northward of her. It was blowing too hard for the Puritan to carry her immense jib-topsail and she took it in. The

Puritan drew ahead rapidly. The wind hauled a little more to northward, and the Genesta took in her spinnaker, jibed over and set it to port. Both boats heretofore had had their spinnakers out to starboard. The Puritan refused to follow her example, and the English boat ran up on her.

The two boats were approaching the outer mark. The Puritan took in her club-topsail. The Genesta passed ahead of the Puritan, taking in her big club-topsail and setting a "jib-header." The Genesta carried her spinnaker well up to the mark; the Puritan took hers in some time before. Now came the windward work. The Genesta clung to her working topsail and carried forestaysail and jib. The Puritan housed her topmast, and with her forestaysail and jib as head sails began to do excellent work. She sailed much dryer than the Genesta. After rounding the stakeboat the yachts stood for a short time on the starboard tack, and then made a long leg to the northward on the port tack. The Puritan passed ahead of the Genesta.

It was when the Genesta came about again on the starboard tack, and stood for the lightship that the hearts of the Americans sank, for the Puritan held her tack and stood so far to the northward that it seemed as if she had forgotten that such a thing as the Scotland Lightship existed.

The Genesta meantime was driving straight for the finish, going at a tremendous pace, and still clinging to her working topsail as if in defiance of the Yankee, who had housed his topmast.

Finally the Puritan came about and stood for the lightship. She kept increasing her windward position until near the finish when she eased her sheets a little and like a flash came down and lapped on to the Genesta's quarter. Then a splendid struggle began. Both yachts seemed to be alive, and both did wonderful work, but steadily the Puritan drew ahead and finally, just before the finish line was reached, gave a great bound ahead and dashed over the line a victor.

It was the most exciting finish ever seen, for nowhere else have two first-class representative yachts contended for so much under such dramatic circumstances. This race settled the possession of the cup for that year. Sir Richard Sutton afterward sailed against the schooner yacht Dauntless for the Cape May and Brenton's Reef cups, and won them. They are now in England, and it is these that the Navahoe hopes to bring back this year. Sir Richard Sutton died in 1891, sincerely mourned by all who knew him and by all the yachtsmen of America.

THE AMERICAN CHAMPION YACHT "PURITAN,"

MODELLED BY EDWARD BURGESS, OF BOSTON, MASS.

Winner of the Two Races for the "America's Cup" against the English Cutter "Genesta" at New York, Sept. 14th and 16th, 1885.

Length Over All, 93 Feet.
   "   On Water Line, 80 Feet.
Beam, 22 Feet 7 Inches.
Draught, 8 Feet 5 Inches.

Length Mast from Deck to Hounds, 60 Feet.
   "   Topmast from Fid to Sheave, 44 Feet.
   "   Bowsprit, Outboard, 38 Feet.
   "   Boom, 76 Feet. Gaff, 47 Feet.

THE GALATEA FAILED, TOO.

SHE WAS NO MATCH FOR THE WONDERFUL MAYFLOWER.

AMERICA EASILY KEPT THE FAMOUS CUP IN
1886 — LIEUTENANT HENN'S GALLANT
STRUGGLE—DETAILS OF THE RACES.

The year after the Genesta raced for the America's Cup, that is in 1886, the Galatea came over and tried her luck. The Galatea was owned and is still owned by Lieutenant Henn, of the Royal Navy, and she was the champion of the Royal Northern Yacht Club. The Galatea did not come with the prestige of the Genesta, as in her racing of the year before in English waters she won only two second prizes out of fifteen starts. She was designed by J. Beaver Webb, the designer of the Genesta, but was not so fast a boat as Sir Richard Sutton's yacht. The Galatea is a

The races of this year showed that Burgess had only begun when he built the Puritan, and that wonderful as that boat seemed he was able to build faster and better boats. This he did when he built the Mayflower, now altered into a schooner, and a fast one. The preliminary arrangements for the races of 1886 were not so diffuse, nor did they cover such a length of time as the correspondence regarding previous races. The same terms were granted to Lieutenant Henn as had been granted to Sir Richard Sutton, and so with a long preface, the Galatea came over in search of the cup.

Meantime the Americans had been preparing to meet the English champion, and although the result showed that the Puritan could have beaten the Galatea, new boats were built to compete in the trial races. From Boston came the Mayflower, built by Burgess at Lawley's yard for General Charles J. Paine. A syndicate of the members of the Atlantic Yacht Club gave a commission to Philip Ellsworth to build a cup defender, and he produced the sloop Atlantic. The owners of the Priscilla still thought she was a boat with a

GALATEA.

good cruising boat, which fact she has amply demonstrated since her defeat in the races for the America's Cup in 1886, but she did not fairly represent the fastest boats of England.

future, and J. Malcolm Forbes knew that the Puritan was one with a history. So these four boats started in the trial races. They had all raced before on the summer cruise of the New-

York Yacht Club, and people generally had "got the measure" of the boats, and knew which was to be the defender of the cup that year. The Galatea had arrived early in the summer at Boston, and joined the New-York Yacht Club fleet at New-Bedford while it was on the annual cruise on August 9. This was the first time the yachtsmen who were to defend the cup had a chance to see the Galatea, and though the record of her races in England was not alarming, yet no one who saw her come sweeping into Buzzard's Bay that day but had a wholesome respect for her. The Tribune of August 10 said:

"As the fleet passed up Buzzard's Bay, a large white cutter with a towering topmast was sighted coming in through Quick's Hole. The blue ensign of the Royal Naval Reserve flying from her peak proclaimed her the Galatea. Before the yachts had all dropped anchor she came gliding into the harbor and anchored near the flagship Electra. As she dropped anchor Commander Gerry hauled down the New-York Yacht Club ensign which had been flying at the fore, and broke out the British blue ensign. At the same time he fired a gun. The Galatea acknowledged the salute, and the flagship ran up the club flag again, while all the yachts in the harbor blazed away a welcome to the Galatea. On the deck of the Galatea were Lieutenant and Mrs. Henn. The Galatea is by no means so pretty as the Genesta, but she is a powerful-looking boat, and has apparently a dangerous amount of 'go' about her."

The Galatea sailed with the New-York Yacht Club fleet for the rest of the cruise, but entered in no races, and carefully avoided any brushes which might enable her qualities to be satisfactorily contrasted with the boats built to defend the cup.

The first of the trial races to select a defender was sailed on August 21. The race was over the New-York Yacht Club's "inside course," the boats entered were the Puritan, Priscilla, Atlantic and Mayflower. This race proved beyond a doubt, if such a doubt existed in the minds of well-informed yachtsmen, that the days of the "rule of thumb" designing had passed and that of scientific yacht-building had succeeded. There never was a better designer of the old school than Philip Ellsworth, the designer of the Atlantic, and never a better sailing master grasped a tiller than his brother "Joe," who sailed her, yet she was a marked failure and had no part in the struggle for supremacy worthy of notice.

The Puritan and the Mayflower taught the Americans not to be afraid of deep draught and outside ballast, and they taught the English the possibilities of the centreboard in sloops of such a size, a lesson which Fife and Watson are still learning, and learning poorly.

The first of the trial races was won by the Mayflower easily. She was not well sailed, but she showed an amount of swiftness which put the possession of the cup beyond a reasonable doubt. That is, to one looking back on it all, and seeing more clearly in the perspective of the past than when incidents were crowding upon each other and the rapid development of yachting was blinding in the rapidity of progress, it was beyond the shadow of a reasonable doubt. But at that time many feared the Galatea, and there was much anxiety about the cup.

An attempt to sail a second trial race was made on August 23, but owing to a brisk wind it was postponed until the next day. The second trial race was sailed over a course 20 miles to leeward and return from the Sandy Hook lightship. The four yachts Puritan, Mayflower, Priscilla and Atlantic started. There was a heavy swell rolling up form the southeast and a good sailing breeze was blowing. The Mayflower won that race with the same ease as she had won the previous one and the committee decided that there was now no necessity of having more trial races, selecting the Mayflower as the American champion that very night. It was decided then that the Galatea and Mayflower should be the two boats to uphold the yachting of their respective countries upon the sea. The dimensions of the two boats were as follows: Galatea, 100 feet over all, 86 feet water-line, 15 feet beam and 13 feet 6 inches draught. Mayflower, 100 feet over all, 85 feet water-line, 23 feet beam and 10 draught.

The first of the races between the two boats was sailed for the great cup on September 7. The course was the New-York Yacht Club course, with the start off Stapleton. The day was a perfect one for a marine pageant and a good one for light-weather racing. A large fleet of yachts and excursion boats came out to see the race and rather interfered with the racers now and then in their anxiety to get near and have a good view of the contest. A light wind was blowing from the south at the start. The signal was given at 10:56 o'clock. The start was one of the prettiest ever seen. The Mayflower was almost on the line, with the Galatea on her weather quarter, when the English yacht suddenly shot ahead and blanketed her rival. They shot over the line together, with only a few seconds difference in their time, and with a speed that was wonderful to behold, the light airs which blew considered.

The Galatea passed ahead of her antagonist and gained a lead which she soon lost. A strong flood tide was running at the start. The yachts crossed on the starboard tack and stood well over to the Long Island shore. They came about on the port tack about the same time, and the Mayflower began to eat out to windward of the Galatea. The British boat seemed to be outfooting the Yankee, but could not point with her at all. The yachts beat down to the Southwest Spit, the Mayflower gaining all the time. At the Southwest Spit Buoy the American yacht was 4 minutes 30 seconds ahead of the British champion. The reach out by the point of the Hook gave a greater margin of safety to the Mayflower, the American boat leading her antagonist at Buoy No. 8 1-2 (old number) by 5 minutes 16 seconds.

The wind outside was from the south-southeast, and the yachts were able to lay a course for the lightship. The wind began to drop as soon as the yachts were over the bar, but after they had rounded the lightship a good breeze sprang up. The long reach out to Sandy Hook lightship was devoid of special interest. The Mayflower increased her lead all the time, and rounded the lightship nearly 10 minutes ahead of the Galatea.

After this there was no race at all, the Galatea never having a chance of catching the Mayflower, and when the yachts had crossed the finish line, just outside the Narrows, the Mayflower was a winner by 12 minutes 40 seconds actual time, and 12 minutes 2 seconds corrected time. The time of the race was as follows:

Name.	Start.	Finish.	Elapsed time.	Corrected time.
Mayflower	10:56:12	4:22:53	5:26:41	5:26:41
Galatea	10:56:11	4:35:32	5:39:21	5:38:43

The course was thirty-eight miles long and the Mayflower allowed the Galatea thirty-eight seconds, according to the rules of the New-York Yacht Club under which the race was sailed.

The second race was put down for contest over an ocean course, twenty miles to windward and return from the Scotland Lightship. There was every prospect of a good race when the

their attendant flotilla of excursion boats groped their way home as best they could. On September 11 the race over the outside course was sailed. The result was a victory for the Mayflower, which was decisive and conclusive, and left no question as to the relative merits of the British and American champions.

When the yachts were started at the Scotland Lightship at 11:20 o'clock the wind was blowing about fifteen miles an hour from the northwest, and the course was therefore laid out twenty miles to the southeast, making the course to leeward and return. The wind, fresh at the start, died out after the outer mark was reached and it seemed at one time as if the race would not be made within the time limit of seven hours. The Mayflower did it, however, and achieved a sweeping victory. The race proved beyond doubt that the Galatea was not a racing boat, and that

THE MAYFLOWER AT THE FINISH.

and the wind died out before the boats had got four miles from the starting point. So the attempted race was a fizzle, and the yachts and yachts were started, but a dense fog shut down

the fears which had been entertained regarding her were groundless. The race was more properly a walkover for the Mayflower, and the Galatea did not get near enough to her in the course of the

THE AMERICAN CHAMPION SLOOP YACHT "MAYFLOWER,"
MODELLED BY EDWARD BURGESS, BOSTON, MASS.
Winner of the Two Races for the "America's Cup" against the English Cutter "Galatea," at New York,
Sept. 7th and 11th, 1886, Winning the First or "Inside" Race by 12 Minutes, 2 Seconds,
and the Second or "Outside" Race by 20 Minutes, 0 Seconds, and Proving
Her Superiority at All Points of Sailing.

race to make the contest interesting. The May-flower won by 20 minutes 48 seconds actual time, and 20 minutes 9 seconds corrected time. The time of the race was as follows:

Name.	Start.	Finish.	Elapsed time.	Corrected time.
Mayflower	11:22:10	0:11:10	6:49:00	6:49:00
Galatea	11:24:10	6:42:58	7:18:48	7:18:09

The Tribune said next morning concerning the defeat of the Galatea:

"Lieutenant Henn, of the Galatea, has had an unpleasant experience, for it is no slight test of any man's equanimity to bring a yacht 3,000 miles and see her beaten at every point in her own weather. But it is some consolation to him to know that his gallantry, courtesy and unfailing good nature have been fully appreciated by American yachtsmen and the American public, and that while it is not in human nature for the victors to refrain from exultation, their rejoicing is tempered by admiration and sympathy for so worthy an antagonist."

Lieutenant Henn and his wife were the recipients of many social courtesies while they remained in the city.

The races of the Galatea were not considered by the English as being at all conclusive as to the relative merits of the American and British type of boats, and before the Galatea had left these waters it was known that a boat was to be built in Scotland which was to come over the next year and make another try for the cup. It began to look as if the British would keep at it year after year until they captured the trophy. This gave a prospect of international yacht racing on this side for many a long year, and the hearts of yachtsmen were glad. No one could see at that time the cloud of the third deed of gift looming above the horizon. The victory of the Puritan in 1885 had established the world-wide reputation of Burgess as a yacht designer, and the victory of the Mayflower confirmed it. He seemed to be America's only designer, and with him the yachtsmen of America felt safe. Orders rushed in on him from all sides, and his fame was such that it not only made his own fortune, but that of the man at whose yards his boats were built. Though the British did not admit that the Galatea was a proper representative champion, they were nevertheless quick to appreciate that the Mayflower was an extremely fast boat, and her influence was not without effect on British yacht designing. Of all the cup defenders the lines of the Mayflower have been perhaps most studied on the other side, and her name is best known. Her name even became popular on the other side, and there are probably half a dozen Mayflowers racing over there to-day.

NOT FOR THE THISTLE.

THE SWIFT SCOTTISH YACHT NOT SWIFT ENOUGH.

SHE COULD NOT TAKE BACK THE AMERICA'S CUP—THE VOLUNTEER, BEST OF BURGESS'S DEFENDERS, WAS A BETTER BOAT.

It was in the year 1887 that the Scottish cutter Thistle came over here in search of the America's Cup. The Thistle came with a great reputation. She was built for the express purpose of sailing for the cup, and she showed in her racing in English waters before she sailed over that she was beyond doubt the fastest yacht in Great Britain; yet she suffered a defeat at the hands of the Volunteer which was so thorough that the English to this day do not believe that the Thistle was sailing in her usual form when the races took place. Lord Dunraven, the present challenger for the cup, says of the Thistle: "Thistle was built for the express purpose of sailing for the cup. She beat Irex on all points of sailing, and was fairly entitled to be considered the champion of the British pleasure fleet of that date. She was badly beaten, so badly as to raise some doubt as to whether she was sailing up to her true form. Taking a line through Thistle, Irex, Genesta on the one hand, and Volunteer, Mayflower, Puritan on the other, she certainly was not. But this is a mere matter of speculation. She was built for the purpose and was the best thing we could turn out."

To defend the cup against the Thistle, Boston and Burgess again were called upon. General Paine, it was generally conceded, was the man to furnish the money for a cup defender, Burgess was the man to design it and Boston was the place for it to be built in. New-York did not even make a struggle for the honor of defending the cup.

General Paine did not feel safe, in view of the Thistle's great reputation, in leaving the defence of the cup to the Mayflower, but decided on building a new boat. Burgess thereupon designed the Volunteer for the General. Trial races were sailed early in September between the Mayflower and the Volunteer, and the latter boat was selected by the special committee of the New-York Yacht Club which had the matter in charge.

The Volunteer is too well known to require an elaborate description. In her present rig of a schooner she can be seen every summer at all the principal regattas. As the Mayflower was faster than the Puritan, so the Volunteer was faster than the Mayflower, and the three cup defenders may be said to have represented the positive, comparative and superlative of Burgess's genius. The Volunteer in those days was of the following dimensions: Length over all, 106.23 feet; water line, 85.88 feet; beam, 23.16 feet; draught, 10 feet. She had 9,000 square feet of sail area, 50 tons of outside ballast and 10 tons of inside ballast. The Thistle was of the following dimensions: Length over all, 108.5 feet;

water line, 86.45 feet; beam, 20.3 feet; draught, 13.8 feet. She had 10 tons of inside ballast and 55 tons in her lead keel.

The correspondence which preceded the international race of 1887 was not so voluminous as usual, a satisfactory arrangement between the New-York Yacht Club and James Bell, the owner of the Thistle, being easily arrived at. The Thistle was designed by Watson, and before she came across started in fifteen races in British waters. In these fifteen races she won eleven first, one second and one third prize. The Thistle arrived in New-York Bay on August 16, and at once there was great popular interest in her. Her owner came over by steamer, arriving soon after the yacht, and at once work was pushed forward on her to get her ready for the ocean fight. She was a boat of such undoubted

Watson and Commodore Bell talked the subject over, amicably arriving at a satisfactory understanding, and the first race was sailed on September 27.

The course was the New-York Yacht Club's old inside course, with the start off Stapleton and the finish at the Narrows. This race was the last one of importance sailed over this course. Both start and finish of the inside course are now outside the Narrows. But even this improved inside course will probably never be again used for an international race. The open ocean beyond Sandy Hook has been chosen as the field for all the contests for the cup this year, and this choice is a precedent which will probably govern in all other international races. The inside course of the New-York Yacht Club was unfair to strangers, but no more so than the course of the Royal

THISTLE.

speed that Americans felt far from certain as to what would be the outcome of the races for the cup, while the Scotch and English, on the other hand, were confident of victory. When the Thistle came to be officially measured for the race it was found that her load water-line length was nearly a foot and a half more than specified in the challenge, when her water-line was announced to be 85 feet. It was declared by some that this invalidated the challenge, but the special committee of the New-York Yacht Club and Mr.

Yacht Squadron, around the Isle of Wight, over which the America originally won the cup.

The race of September 28 was a glorious victory for the Volunteer. The American sloop beat the Scottish cutter 19 minutes 23 1-4 seconds, and as the finish was with spinnakers set and a fair working breeze blowing, this represented a greater distance than had ever before at a finish been between the two contestants for this trophy. The Thistle hardly deserved so bad a beating. She would have been defeated any way, but ill luck made her defeat a bad one. It was fluky weather during the first part of the race, the wind constantly shifting and each change favoring the American yacht. Both yachts were much bothered by tugs and excursion steamers which crowded about them, for all New-York seemed to have gone down to see the contest, and all New-York is a nuisance when it is at a yacht race.

The yachts went over the line at low water slack, with a light air from the south southeast, the Thistle in the lead, with the Volunteer on her weather quarter a couple of points. They crossed on the port tack and stood over toward Staten Island. The Thistle came about after a little and stood for the Long Island shore, her sailing master, Captain Barr, not being aware that over under the Staten Island shore a slight drain of ebb tide was still running. Captain Haff, the sailing master of the Volunteer, knew this, however, being familiar with these waters, and aware of the fact that there is a difference of nearly an hour in the time of the turning of the tide on the Long Island and Staten Island shores. So he did not allow himself to be forced about by the Thistle, but kept off under her stern and stood for the Staten Island shore.

Meantime the Thistle over on the Long Island shore was getting the young flood on her weather beam. When she came about on the port tack and the Volunteer came on the starboard the two yachts approached each other in midchannel, and it was evident that the Thistle had lost her lead. She could not weather the Volunteer and was forced about under the Yankee sloop's lee bow, being blanketed at the same time and hanging helpless. Then in a trice the wind hauled from south southeast to south southwest, giving the Volunteer a nice slant along the Staten Island shore, while for two or three minutes the Scottish cutter lay becalmed, and the Volunteer led her by six minutes through the Narrows.

Opening out the Lower Bay the Volunteer caught the freshening breeze and still further increased her lead. It was evident that the Thistle was a beaten boat already, and all the steamboats and tugs and all the people on them made joyful noises. The wind subsequently backed to south southeast, and the Volunteer got that first, so that at the Southwest Spit the American boat had a commanding lead, which she preserved with ease to the finish. In the run from the Lightship the Thistle gained a trifle, but not much. The time of the race was as follows:

	Start.	Finish.	Elapsed Time.	Corrected Time.
Volunteer	12:31:53¾	5:28:16¼	4:53:18	4:53:18
Thistle	12:32:06	5:45:52¾	5:12:46¾	5:12:41¾

This race was witnessed by a company both large and distinguished. The Secretaries of State and the Navy came to see it, and on both sides of the Atlantic the wires kept people informed of the progress of the yachts over the course. To say that Scotland and England were surprised at the result is to put it mildly; they were astonished. Why the Britons were so astonished it is difficult to see. They have been sending boats over here for many years to race for the cup, and each time they are defeated they seem more and more surprised. The defeat of the Thistle was unexpectedly overwhelming, even to Americans, and there were all sorts of rumors started that something had been done to the yacht's bottom by evil-minded persons. They were entirely without foundation, however, the great Watson being responsible for everything pertaining to the underwater body of the Thistle before and after the races.

The rapid bound, or rather bounds, which American yacht building had made in three yachts, taking three steps from nadir to zenith, proved so astounding that even Americans could scarcely comprehend what had happened. It is hardly to be expected that the English would have done so. Mr. Bell, the owner of the Thistle, said after the race:

"The course is a miserable one. It is the worst of which I have had any experience. Had I known it was so bad the Thistle would never have been built. We were simply out-lucked yesterday, and we did not have a fair show."

Then Mr. Bell had the bottom of the Thistle swept carefully with ropes to see if there was any foreign substance attached to her bottom which had been put there by designing Americans. When it was found that the Thistle's bottom was as the designer had made it, there was more wonder, and all the crew, together with the owner and designer, went about in that state of mind so graphically described by Bret Harte:

> "Do I sleep; do I dream?
> Is things what they seem,
> Or is visions about?"

The English papers as a rule took the defeat philosophically. "The London Daily News" said in the course of a long article: "The Thistle has been beaten in a wind that was, so to speak, of her own choosing. She never had a chance from the start or, to be quite accurate, from the first five minutes which followed the start. We had better drain our cup of bitterness to the dregs. It is idle to deny it. What will account for it?"

"The London Standard" in its editorial said: "We would much rather have won. But if we are to be beaten we would rather it should be by America than any other country."

"The Daily Telegraph" said: "Time and time again we have sought to push into the first place naturally belonging to us as the mistress of the seas, but as often has our champion returned discomfited and cast down."

In Paris on the day of the race the betting was heavy, and many thousands of dollars changed hands. In all the poolrooms and clubs of the French capital bets were made freely, and the odds given were in favor of the Thistle. But there was another race yet to be sailed and the Thistle was to have a chance over the outside course. So mustering what hope they could the Scotchmen went out to the Scotland Lightship on September 29 to meet the Volunteer. There was no wind on that day, however, and the race was postponed until September 30. On that day the two champions sailed a race twenty miles to windward and return from the Scotland Lightship. The result was the defeat of the Thistle by 11 minutes, 48 3-4 seconds. This probably is a just standard to take in comparing the two boats, and shows exactly how much better the Volunteer was than the Thistle. No element of luck or local pilot knowledge entered in the victory. There was a moderate whole-sail breeze blowing and the course was within a point of dead to windward. The wind held steady most of the time. For five or ten minutes after the second tack, when the yachts were beating off shore, the wind dropped a bit and shifted from east to southeast, but this was in favor of the Thistle rather than the Volunteer, and the breeze soon sprang up again from its original quarter. The Volunteer gained from the start and it was soon evident to all who looked on that she was a sure

on the part of Lord Duraven and those who now direct the policy of the New-York Yacht Club, that a long discussion of the instrument would be out of place here. Those who drew up the deed seem to have an idea that it would foster international yacht racing. As a matter of fact it stopped it for six years and brought much criticism upon American yachtsmen.

Soon after the defeat of the Thistle the America's Cup was returned to George L. Schuyler, the surviving member of the syndicate which owned the America, and he gave it back to the New-York Yacht Club under the third "deed of gift," an instrument which had been prepared for his signature by members of the club. The celebrated

THE VOLUNTEER IN THE HOMESTRETCH.

winner. In the windward work the Volunteer was superb. The Thistle was nowhere compared with her.

Running home the Thistle made better time than the Volunteer, but never stood any chance of saving the day. This race, of course, settled the question of the possession of the cup. The time of the race was as follows:

	Start.	Finish.	Elapsed Time.	Corrected Time.
Volunteer	10:40:50¼	4:23:47	5:42:56¾	5:42:56¾
Thistle	10:40:21	4:35:12	5:54:51	5:54:45

Upon this, the latest race for the cup, followed close a thing which threatened for a time to put an end forever to these time-honored and honorable international contests. That was the third "deed of gift." So much had been written about it, so disastrous did it prove to international racing, and so completely have its iniquities been overcome by moderation and sportsmanlike conduct

instrument is a long document, full of legal verbiage. There is a lot about parties of the first and second parts and "transfer and set over and by these presents does grant." The clause in the deed which occasioned the most criticism is one known as the "dimension clause." This clause is as follows:

"The challenging club shall give ten months notice in writing, naming the days for the proposed races; but no races shall be sailed in the days intervening between November 1 and May 1. Accompanying the ten months' notice of challenge there must be sent the name of the owner and a certificate of the rig and following dimensions of the challenging vessel, namely: Length on load-water line, beam at load-water line, extreme beam and draught of water, which dimensions shall not be exceeded, and a custom house registry of the vessel must be sent as soon as possible."

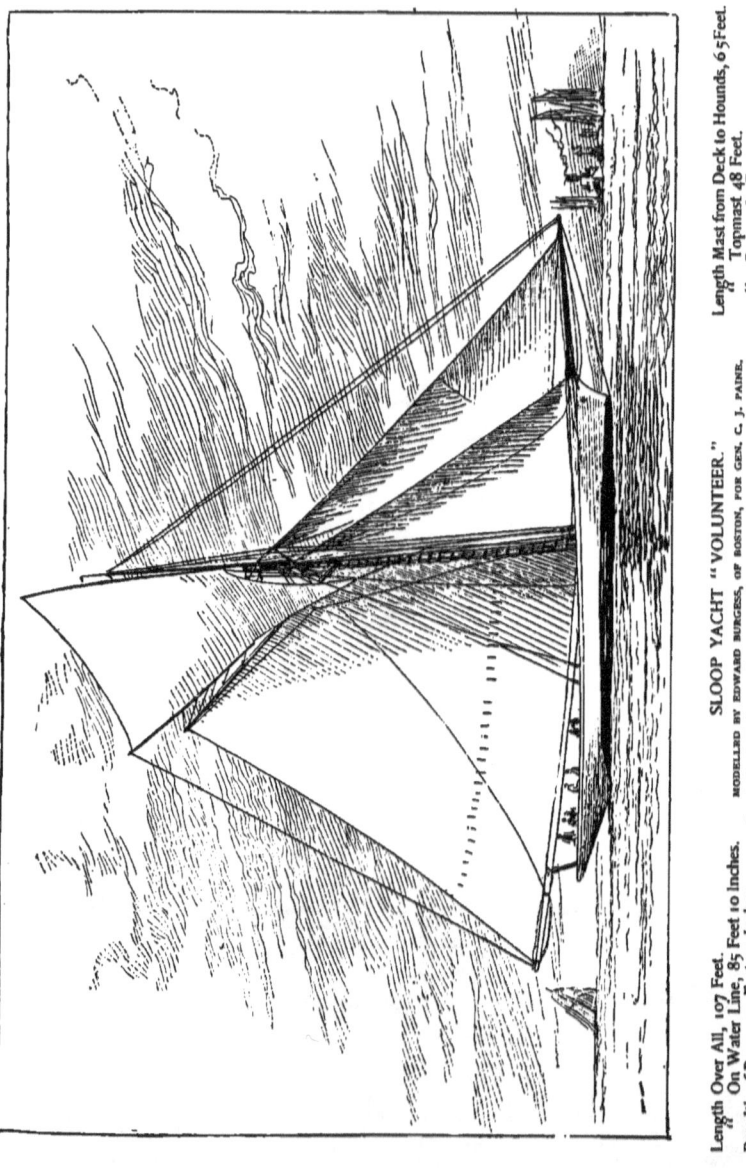

SLOOP YACHT "VOLUNTEER."

MODELLED BY EDWARD BURGESS, OF BOSTON, FOR GEN. C. J. PAINE.

Steel Hull Built by Pusey & Jones, Wilmington, Del. Spars by
Geo. Lawley & Son, South Boston. Sails by Wilson &
Griffin, New York.

Length Over All, 107 Feet.
" On Water Line, 85 Feet 10 Inches.
Breadth of Beam, 23 Feet 10 Inches.
Depth of Hold, 10 Feet 6 Inches.
Draft, 10 Feet 9 Inches.

Length Mast from Deck to Hounds, 65 Feet.
" Topmast 48 Feet.
" Boom, 84 Feet.
" Gaff, 52 Feet.
" Bowsprit, Outboard, 37 Feet.

FOR THE RACE OF 1893.

NEGOTIATIONS WHICH LED TO THE CHALLENGE FOR THE AMERICA'S CUP.

LORD DUNRAVEN'S PATIENCE AND PERSEVERANCE—CONDITIONS WHICH GOVERN THE INTERNATIONAL MATCH.

A considerable change had taken place in 1892 in the feelings of the members of the New-York Yacht Club regarding the latest deed of gift. The leading members of the club saw that a strict insistence upon all the terms of the deed would act as a bar to future challenges for the America's Cup. Lord Dunraven, who had travelled extensively in America and was well acquainted with many American yachtsmen, had tried unsuccessfully two years before to get the club to waive the dimensions clause of the deed with a view to challenging for the cup. He was well aware that a change had taken place in the sentiment of the club, and one night H. Maitland Kersey remarked to a group of yachtsmen assembled at the clubhouse that he felt justified in saying that Lord Dunraven was still anxious for a race, and would challenge if satisfactory arrangements regarding the terms of a race could be made. The result of Mr. Kersey's "sounding" of the club was such that he reported to Lord Dunraven that in his opinion a match could be arranged on terms satisfactory to both sides.

A LETTER FROM LORD DUNRAVEN.

Lord Dunraven then wrote to J. V. S. Oddie, secretary of the New-York Yacht Club, saying that he would send over a formal challenge for the cup, provided he was not required to give the dimensions of his yacht other than her length on the load-water line and her custom-house tonnage. He desired that five races be sailed, and that neither the challenging yacht nor the defender should exceed her estimated length by more than 2 per cent, and should pay double for any excess of estimated length in penalty of time allowance. He also made as a condition of challenging that it should be understood, should the cup be won by his boat, that it should be held by the yacht club into the custody of which it would pass subject to challenge upon exactly the same conditions as those under which it was won. This was an ignoring of the deed of gift, but the New-York Yacht Club held a special meeting to consider Lord Dunraven's propositions. At this meeting it was argued by General Charles J. Paine that in the mutual agreement clause of the deed of gift a liberal course might be pursued regarding the conditions of a match, and a committee of which the General was made chairman was appointed to arrange a race with Lord Dunraven "in accordance with the terms of the last deed of gift."

REPLY OF THE COMMITTEE.

The committee sent a letter to the Earl in which, while the deed of gift was insisted on as being the only law governing races for the America's cup, it was also pointed out that the mutual agreement clause of the deed would allow a race to be sailed on the terms proposed by his lordship. It was insisted, however, that in case the cup passed, by reason of a victory by Lord Dunraven, to the custody of another club, it must be held according to the terms of the deed of gift. Here was a hitch, and for a while it looked like no race.

Mr. Kersey, as representative of Lord Dunraven, had a consultation with the committee, and it was pointed out to him that in case he won the cup the club obtaining the custody of it could, under the mutual agreement clause, make any sort of arrangement it pleased regarding races for it except that it must be always bound to accept a challenge made according to the rules laid down in the deed of gift. Lord Dunraven wrote at once to say that this was satisfactory.

A NEW QUESTION COMES UP.

His letter, however, which he had intended to settle everything, raised a new question, and gave an opening for more negotiations, for in it he spoke of the first and second deeds of gift, putting them on a parity with the latest deed and saying that no challenge made under the conditions laid down in any of the deeds would be refused. The committee telegraphed him that it would recommend the New-York Yacht Club to accept a challenge on the lines laid down by him if he would withdraw his reference to the first and second deeds of gift. He telegraphed, "References to former deeds of gift withdrawn." The secretary of the Royal Yacht Squadron, Richard Grant, telegraphed that he had forwarded by mail a formal challenge for the America's Cup on behalf of Lord Dunraven.

On the night of December 13, the challenge having arrived, a special meeting of the New-York Yacht Club was held to consider its acceptance, and to hear the report of the special committee which had been intrusted with the negotiations regarding the challenge. Great interest was taken in the meeting. Although it was pretty certain that the challenge would be accepted, yet so many hitches have always taken place in negotiations for races for the America's Cup that no one could be absolutely sure that the season of 1893 would see a race for the celebrated trophy until the club had actually and formally accepted the challenge. Over 200 members attended the meeting.

THE CHALLENGE'S CONDITIONS.

The text of the challenge laid before the meeting was as follows:

Royal Yacht Squadron Castle, Cowes, Isle of Wight, November 25, 1892.

To Secretary J. V. S. Oddie:

I am requested by Lord Dunraven to forward to you a formal challenge for the cup, on the following conditions, which I understand have been agreed upon between Lord Dunraven and a committee appointed by the New-York Yacht Club to conduct negotiations and arrange all the details, viz.:

Conditions agreed upon between Lord Dunraven and a committee of the New-York Yacht Club and contained in Lord Dunraven's letters of September 16 to Mr. Oddie, and of November 7 to General Paine.

First—Length of load-water line of challenging vessel to be the only dimension required, this to be sent with the challenge and the Custom-House register to follow as soon as possible.

Second—Any excess over estimated length of loadwater line to count double in calculating time allowance, but the challenging vessel not to exceed, in any case, such estimated length by more than two percentage; the yacht that sails against the challenging vessel not to exceed the estimated length of the loadwater line of the challenging vessel more than two percentage, and any excess of length beyond the estimated length of challenging vessel in loadwater line to count double in calculating time allowance;

THE EARL OF DUNRAVEN.

provided that no yacht of specific rig existing or under construction October 20, 1892, and available for use by the New-York Yacht Club in defending the cup, be barred or penalized beyond taking or giving ordinary time allowance according to the New-York Yacht Club rules.

Third—It is understood and agreed that should the cup come into the custody of a British yacht club it shall be held subject to challenge under precisely similar terms as those contained in this challenge; provided, always, that such club shall not refuse any challenge according to the conditions laid down in the deed of 1887.

I, therefore, in behalf of the Royal Yacht Squadron, and in the name of Lord Dunraven, a member of the squadron, challenge to sail a series of matches with the yacht Valkyrie against any one yacht or vessel constructed in the United States, for the America Cup, and would suggest that the match be sailed in August or September, 1893. Lord Dunraven would be glad if the precise dates can be left open for the time, but if your committee so desire he will name the exact date on hearing from them. The following are particulars of the challenging vessel.

Owner, Lord Dunraven; name, Valkyrie; length, loadwater line, 85 feet. Custom-House measurement will follow as soon as the vessel can be measured for registration. Shall be much obliged if you will send your replying letter soon so that the matter can be laid before the committee.   RICHARD GRANT.

THE REPORT ACCEPTED.

The special committee recommended that the challenge be accepted, and made an elaborate report of the negotiations which it had so successfully conducted. The report was accepted, and the committee continued to arrange further details regarding the match. The next day the Royal Yacht Squadron was officially informed of the acceptance of the challenge.

The negotiations which resulted in the challenge began with Lord Dunraven's letter of September 16 to Mr. Oddie, and ended with the acceptance of the challenge on December 13, a space of nearly three months of constant correspondence. The special committee which brought the negotiations to a successful issue was composed of General Charles J. Paine, James D. Smith, A. Cass Canfield, Archibald Rogers and Latham A. Fish. This result was not obtained without considerable pressure being brought to bear to prevent it on both sides of the water.

A considerable party of British yachtsmen were opposed to having a challenge for the cup sent over as long as the New-York Yacht Club adhered to the deed of gift. The British press was generally opposed to any arrangement being arrived at which did not involve an entire repudiation of the deed of gift on the part of the New-York Yacht Club, and Lord Dunraven was urged to break off the negotiations. On this side of the water there were yachtsmen who desired a rigid insistence upon the terms of the deed of gift, and some who desired to see it abolished. Lord Dunraven and the committee, however, worked along quietly, and the result of their work satisfied everybody worth satisfying. It being settled that there was to be a race, Lord Dunraven gave an order to Watson, the English designer, for a boat of the required dimensions.

NAMING THE NEW BOAT VALKYRIE.

Lord Dunraven's old boat with which he had vainly sought to arrange a match was called the Valkyrie, and so the new boat was also named Valkyrie. She was launched from the shipyards at Gourock, Scotland, early in 1893, and accounts of her trial spins have been frequently sent over here. She is said to be a better all-around boat than those of the same class built to defend the Royal Victoria Cup against the American yacht Navahoe. No effort has been spared to make her the fastest boat of her class in the British yachting fleet. Until she has raced

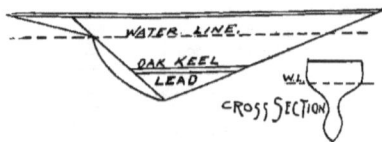

THE LINES OF THE VALKYRIE.

more, however, nothing definite can be known as to her qualities of speed.

On this side of the water as soon as the race was settled upon, orders were given for the building of four boats from which to select a defender of the cup. Two syndicates were formed in New-York, one headed by Archibald Rogers, and the other by Commodore E. D. Morgan, of the New-York Yacht Club. These syndicates placed their orders with Herreshoff, the Bristol designer and builder.

Two boats were ordered from Boston, both of the fin keel type—one by General Charles J. Paine and son, and designed by J. B. Paine; the other by a syndicate, the boat being designed by Stewart and Binney.

THE VALKYRIE.

THE VALKYRIE A FINE BOAT.

WHAT THE ENGLISH CUP-SEEKER LOOKS LIKE —HER OVER-MEASUREMENTS.

The best picture of the Valkyrie which has reached this side of the water is the one herewith given. The performances of Lord Dunraven's yacht in her races on the other side have proved that in sending her over to race for the America's Cup England sends her fastest yacht. The English regard the Genesta and Thistle as the only really representative sloops which have come over here to race for the America's Cup. It would seem that if the Valkyrie is defeated there would be no chance for a claim that she was not thoroughly a representative of the best yachting genius of Great Britain. The new measurements of the Valkyrie recently made were startling in that they showed a waterline of 86.82 feet, instead of 85 feet, the length she was supposed to have on the water-line and the length specified in the challenge and the agreement for the international race. According to the compact regarding the races for the cup entered into between the New-York Yacht Club and the Royal

Yacht Squadron both challenger and defender were limited absolutely to an excess of 2 per cent over the specified length of 85 feet. Every inch in excess of the specified length is to be counted double in computing time allowance. A sailing length computed on the present waterline of the Valkyrie would, in view of the double penalty, seriously interfere with her chances of winning, provided the defender was of the specified length on waterline and the race a close one. It is announced that the Valkyrie's spars have been reduced and other alterations made in her which will bring her just within the limit.

By the time the Valkyrie reaches these shores she is likely to have again increased her load-waterline length, as she is a composite yacht and such boats always increase in length and displacement a little after two or three months' immersion. By the use of the adze and by the stripping of inside fittings she can undoubtedly be brought back to the limit, however. It is by no means certain that the cup defenders will not be found to have the same trouble as the Valkyrie and alterations may have to be made in them to bring them to the 85-foot waterline.

THE FOUR DEFENDERS.

BOATS WHICH HAVE BEEN BUILT TO BATTLE FOR THE CUP.

VIGILANT, JUBILEE, COLONIA AND PILGRIM—
THE SPECIAL FEATURES OF EACH—
THE FIN-KEEL CONTROVERSY.

As soon as the arrangements for the international races had been completed the question of a boat to defend the cup came up. Two syndicates were promptly formed in New-York and one in Boston, and General Paine announced that his

Phelps Carroll to cross the ocean in search of the Royal Victoria and the Cape May and Brenton's Reef cups. Herreshoff built for the Morgan-Iselin syndicate the sloop Vigilant, and for the Rogers syndicate the sloop Colonia.

The Boston syndicate placed its orders for a cup-defender with Stewart & Binney, the successors to the business of Burgess. Mr. Paine designed his own boat and had her built at South Boston.

Of the four boats thus built the two Boston boats are fin-keels, the Stewart & Binney boat being purely a fin-keel and the Paine boat a fin-keel centreboard. Of the two boats built at Herreshoff's the Morgan-Iselin boat was a power-

THE VIGILANT.

son, John B. Paine, would build a boat to compete for the honor of defending the trophy. The principal shareholders in one of the New-York syndicates were C. Oliver Iselin and Commodore E. D. Morgan, of the New-York Yacht Club. The other New-York syndicate was headed by Archibald Rogers. Both these syndicates placed their orders with the Herreshoffs, who already had under way the Navahoe, building for Royal

ful centreboard sloop and the Rogers boat a keel sloop. By the end of June all the boats were in the water, and their owners, designers and sailing-masters began to tune them up. The Morgan-Iselin syndicate boat was named the Vigilant. Though the Vigilant shows in her model those general Herreshoff characteristics so well exemplified in the lines of the Gloriana and Wasp, she is a departure from the general model of those in many vital particulars. She is a perfect exemplification of the idea of power in boat-building. Her dimensions are as follows: Length over all, 128 feet; load-waterline, 85 feet; beam, 26 feet; draught, 14 feet. The Vigilant has a large sail plan, and to make her stand up under it her large beam is assisted by seventy-five tons of ballast. So great a combination of beam and depth in an 85-footer has never before been attempted. Her midship section is rather full, with a round, easy bilge. She is an experiment, not only in her combinations of elements of power and speed, but also in her material, being plated with Tobin bronze up to her top streak, which is of steel. Tobin bronze, it is declared, will not rust and is hard to foul. It is light and strong and gives a smooth surface such as cannot be obtained on a steel boat. If the Vigilant is a success in regard to the material of which she is constructed it is probable that many future racers will be built of Tobin bronze.

sailing in every regatta of importance so as to get used to the excitement of a yacht race and work together in it. The speed shown by the Vigilant has been great, as has indeed that shown by all the boats built for cup defenders.

The sailing-master of the Vigilant is William Hansen. He is a Norwegian, forty-six years old. He went to sea when seventeen years old and began yachting on this side of the water in 1870 in the schooner Alice. He was formerly the sailing-master of the schooner Sachem and in her won many races.

The Rogers syndicate boat was named the Colonia when she was launched. She is built of steel and is a typical Herreshoff keel boat. She is not so startling in her design as the other cup defenders, the designers seemingly having tried to reproduce in her all the virtues of the Gloriana and the Wasp. She has the graceful reversed curves seen in the Wasp at the stem, while her sternpost has a moderate rake. She carries her

JUBILEE.

The centreboard of the Vigilant is made of thin plates of bronze and is hollow. It is 17 feet long and 10 feet deep. The boom of the Vigilant is the one built for the schooner Constellation when Commodore Morgan thought of changing that boat into a sloop. The boom is 98 feet long. The crew of the Vigilant was carefully selected, and before the yacht was ready for them the men were practised every day on the schooner Iroquois,

body well forward and aft, and is sharper at the bows than the Wasp. She has a fulness aft which gives her great power at that point when she heels. There are fifty tons of outside ballast on her keel. Her dimensions are: Length over all, 126 feet; load-waterline, 85 feet; beam, 24 feet; draught, 15 feet 6 inches.

After the Colonia had been sailed about in Narraganset Bay and off Newport she was brought to

New-York and placed in drydock, where New-York yachtsmen had for the first time a chance to see her under-water body. She certainly gave an idea of great speed, produced by fine lines and scientific designing. The most critical could not call her a "freak" or a "racing machine." She is a yacht legitimately evolved along certain well-defined lines. An interesting thing about the Colonia is that she is sailed by the famous skipper "Hank" Haff, who sailed the Volunteer against the Thistle in the cup races of 1887. Captain Haff was born at Islip, L. I., sixty-two years ago. He is a most skilful sailing-master, as every one interested in yachting knows, and age has not yet begun to decrease his powers of seamanship or blunt the keenness of his love for the sport and dash of a yacht race. Captain Haff has been to sea since he was a boy, either in the merchant

through the canals to New-York, where her fin-plate was put on in drydock at the Erie Basin. She is a singular-looking boat out of water, and even those hardened to the fin-keels of Boston could not look at her without wonder. Her hull is in sharp contrast to that of an ordinary sailing vessel. From it extends straight down for seventeen feet her big steel fin. Well forward she has a little centreboard. It is not exactly a centreboard either, for it is not in the usual place of a centreboard, nor is it intended to perform the functions of a centreboard. It is a movable plate sliding down through the bottom of the boat about where the forefoot would be if she had a forefoot, and is intended to help balance the boat steering.

The dimensions of the Pilgrim are: 120 feet over all, 85 feet load-waterline, 23 feet beam, 5 feet draught of hull, 17 feet depth of fin and 22

PILGRIM.

service or in the yachting fleet. Among other places he held was that of sailing-master of the sloop-yacht Fannie in the days when she was a great racer. Under his handling the Fannie won nine first prizes out of eleven starts.

The Stewart & Binney boat was built of steel at Wilmington, Del., by Pusey & Jones. She was named the Pilgrim when she was launched. After being put in the water she was taken

feet total draught. She has a long, sharp prow. From full outlines at the midship section her sheer and keel lines converge rapidly and join in a sharp point under the bowsprit. The lines abaft the midship section are full, but fall away rapidly and end in a sharp and shallow overhang astern. The Pilgrim has a good side to sail on. She will carry twenty tons of ballast and have a larger sail spread than did the Volunteer.

The question of so building a boat of the size of the Pilgrim as to render the great leverage of the fin harmless is one which before the building of the two big Boston fin-keel cup defenders designers had been loath to meet. Boston regards the fin-keel, however, as a thing of its own and one to be encouraged, so when it came to the cided that hers should be fin-keels, and Paine and Stewart & Binney faced the problems of construction boldly. The great draught of the fin-keels, however, will probably, if nothing else does, preclude the use of the types in boats of this size. The Pilgrim, for instance, draws twenty-two feet of water. This is about the draught of a good-sized ocean steamer. The Pilgrim is an extreme type of fin-keel, and in her construction speed only has been considered. Her sail plan will not be abnormally large.

The Paine boat was named the Jubilee when she was launched because, General Paine said, this year was the American year of jubilee. She is built of steel and has a fin-keel like the Pilgrim. More than that, she has two centreboards, a little one up forward under the bows, just as the Pilgrim has, and one big one dropping down through the fin. Her fin has a lead bulb on it and extends down eight feet from the hull. As the hull draws 5 feet 7 inches, this gives the Jubilee a total draught of 13 feet 7 inches. The fin is of steel plates and the bulb of lead at the bottom weighs thirty-five tons The big centreboard is of steel and weighs two and one-half tons. It is 10 feet long and 7 feet deep. The smaller centreboard is of steel also. It is only 3 feet wide, but it drops straight down for 8 feet.

The boom of the Jubilee is 95 feet long and she carries a big spread of canvas. She is 85 feet on the water-line and 22 feet 6 inches beam. The Jubilee carries out to some extent the idea of power of which General Paine was always fond. Power, however, has not been overdone apparently in Jubilee, the General probably having a remembrance of the Alboruk, which was all power and little speed.

The Jubilee has good underwater lines, and in sailing goes through the water easily. There is no hollow to the water along her waist, and consequently no suction. She steers with remarkable ease, her little centreboard under her bow no doubt helping her immensely in this. The Jubilee will be sailed by John Barr, the well-known sailing-master. John Barr and Charles Barr have both fine reputations as sailors of racing yachts. John Barr is a Scotchman by birth and came over here as sailingmaster of the Thistle in 1887. He was born at Gourock and passed his boyhood in sailing and building boats on the Clyde. Captain Barr made a reputation on the other side long before he came over here. After he sailed the Thistle in the cup races of 1887 he returned to Scotland in her. He rather liked this country, however, and came back here to take charge of the Clara. Now he is naturalized and will stay here. Among the yachts of which Captain Barr has had charge are the Gloriana, Clara, May, Thistle and Cinderella.

The Stewart & Binney boat will be sailed by Captain Sherlock, a sailing-master of renown. The date of the first of the trial races to select a defender for the cup has been fixed for September 7. On that day these four boats, of which brief descriptions have here been given, will come out on the open sea to do battle for the honor of defending the great cup. They are all fleet yachts, well manned and in charge of competent sailing-masters. That these new yachts are much faster than the Volunteer cannot be doubted. To look at the Volunteer's lines now, and then at those of the cup defenders, even a novice can see the greater development of speed. Yet it was only a few years ago that the Volunteer was the fastest boat in the world. There is, of course, great divergence of opinion among yachtsmen regarding the types represented in the four cup defenders. To a conservative mind the advent of fin-keels of the size of the Jubilee and Pilgrim comes with something like a shock. Some prejudiced people

even go so far as to say that they would rather the cup went over to the other side in the locker of the Valkyrie than to have it retained here by the victory of a fin-keel. On the other hand, the advocates of the fin-keel type say that there is no reason for the prejudice against the fin-keel. A fin-keel, they say, is simply a deep-keel boat with the deadwood cut away. They maintain that a fin-keel boat of the size of the Jubilee or Pilgrim can be constructed, the life of which will be just as long as that of a keel or centreboard boat of the same size.

That part of the yachting world which once loved the skimming dish and gave up their idol reluctantly are in favor of the type represented by the Vigilant. Not that there is anything of the skimming dish about her, for she has a draught which would preclude that, but there is the idea of power carried to its fullest extent and of beam as a help to the carrying of the great sails. Then, above all, she has a centreboard.

The Colonia represents a conservative development of ideas, based on the great success of the Wasp and Gloriana. She has a large following of those who do not believe in extreme power but in fineness of lines as a means of speed. The idea of power, however, is not wanting in any of the cup defenders, and reports from the other side show that the English designers have been run-

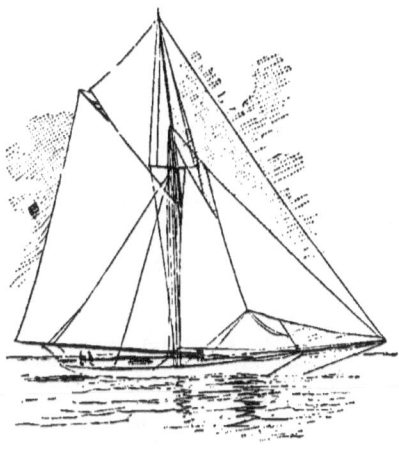

COLONIA.

ning to power to a degree hitherto unprecedented over there. It is a good thing that this year the defence of the cup was not left entirely to Boston. The building of two boats by New-York yachtsmen and of two by Boston yachtsmen to compete for the honor of defending the cup has encouraged a spirit of friendly rivalry between the two cities which cannot but result in the advancement of yachts, for the more rivalry the more races, and the more races the better yachts. For the last three times the cup has been sailed for Boston has defended it, and it is worthy of note that of the four cup defenders this year all were designed and three were built in New-England. It is not probable that New-York will rest until the scientific centre of yacht-building and designing is restored to her. It went East when Burgess appeared, and Herreshoff keeps it there.

The dimensions given here of the cup defenders are only approximate, the boats not having been officially measured, up to the time of going to press.

VIGILANT AND JUBILEE.

A RACE OVER THE SOUND FROM NEW-LONDON TO NEWPORT.

BUT THE HERRESHOFF FLYER CAME IN AHEAD AND BOSTON'S PARTISANS WERE SORRY THAT ROGER WILLIAMS HAD EVER BEEN BANISHED TO RHODE ISLAND —TWO WONDERS OF THE SEA—ANOTHER GREAT RACE TO-DAY.

[BY TELEGRAPH TO THE TRIBUNE.]

Newport, Aug. 10.—For the first time two of the cup-defenders have been brought together in a set race. It was on the run from New-London to this port, and though the relative merits of the two boats were not fully tested it affords great opportunity to observe their qualities in light winds on certain points of sailing. The interest in the run was all with the cup-defenders, and the big fleet of fast schooners and sloops, which in ordinary times would have attracted the attention of all who loved yachting, and have aroused a feeling of admiration even in those who do not comprehend the qualities of a yacht and the science of her construction and her sailing, were almost unnoticed in the general desire to learn about the two big sloops, Vigilant and Jubilee. These two boats built to defend the great "blue ribbon of the sea," the America's Cup, swept with their towers of canvas from New-London to Newport, blown along at the head of the fleet under a gentle southwest wind which swelled their immense sails and, even in the light air, sent them down along the low-lying shores of Rhode Island at a rate which filled the observers with wonder, until under the waveworn rocks of Fort Dumpling the race was finished. It was a wonderful exhibition of speed and showed how the science of yachtbuilding has advanced by great bounds. Where were the fleet boats of last year and the year before? Back in the "ruck," their fame forgotten and their speed as naught. Only the steam yachts were the worthy competitors of those two magnificent sloops which rushed along over the shining water grand and majestic and unapproachable. The stories which have been told of the cup-defenders having had brushes with steam vessels in their practice sails have been received with ridicule by almost everybody. Those who saw the Vigilant and the Jubilee sail to-day were willing to believe the wildest tales that would be told of their prowess on the seas.

Year after year has brought its surprises in yachting since first the Puritan pushed across the seas. It seemed each time as if the limit of speed in a sailing vessel had been reached; but science has overleaped experience and each year has produced its wonder. The last and crowning glory of human skill in shipbuilding has been reached in the cup-defenders.

Whether the Jubilee or the Vigilant won in to-day's race cannot be known until the yachts are officially measured. The Vigilant overtook the Boston boat and passed her shortly before the finish, but she came in ahead by such a small margin that it may be that the Jubilee won on time allowance. Even the benefit of time allowance would not save the victory to the Jubilee if it were not for the fact that it was a one-gun start for the two big sloops, their time being taken from the time of gun fire, and not at the actual time they crossed the line. The Jubilee crossed fully a minute ahead of the Vigilant; but that, under the circumstances, did not count to her favor in computing her time. However, it is not of so much importance which boat had the technical advantage in the race. The main fact, standing out clear as did the towering sails of the majestic sloops on the sparkling surface of the sea, is that boats have been produced on this side of the water which in all human probability make the American nation still mistress of the yachting seas. The art of prophecy has fallen into disuse in this twilight of the nineteenth century, and no oracle sits on the rocks of Beaver Tail to tell of what will be the result of the conflict with Valkyrie, but to all who saw the Vigilant and Jubilee sail yesterday the quest of Lord Dunraven seemed a hopeless one.

Four of the cup-defenders will to-morrow contend for the Goelet Cup over a course outside the harbor, and all New-England has poured thousands of people into Rhode Island to see the race. Steamers, tugs and steam yachts have been chartered all along the coast. For one excursion steamer alone 800 tickets have been sold in Boston. The interest in the coming international contest which is felt in New-York is faint and languid compared with the intense feeling regarding it felt in this section of the country.

The morning rose over the ocean serene and fair to-day, and all the great fleet anchored in the harbor of New-London shone in the splendor of the new-born day. When at 10 o'clock a gun from the flagship May gave the preparatory signal the foretops of barren masts blossomed out in snowy canvas, anchors were weighed and the fleet poured out of the harbor down toward where, off Sarah's Ledge, the flagship May had taken up a position to time the yachts.

At 10:10 the big sloops were started. The Jubilee was over the line first, and about a minute behind her came the Vigilant. Each yacht had a jib-topsail up and carried forestaysail and jib. The two yachts stood down toward Race Rock, and by the time that mark was reached the Boston boat was about three-quarters of a mile ahead of the Vigilant. Then began the jubilation of Boston people, and the hearts of the New-Yorkers sank deep down. It did not seem possible that the Vigilant could close up that great gap of glittering, shining water between her and her antagonist. Behind them came the rest of the fleet, moving slowly down in the light wind and forming a beautiful marine pageant. The sloops, other than the cup-defenders, were started at 10:15, and the schooners at 10:20. It was a one-gun start for the cup-defenders only, the other yachts being timed after the usual manner. The cup-defenders had a one-gun start because the trial races and the international races will be sailed in the same manner, and it was desired to give the crews experience in such starts, where advantage of position when the starting gun is fired is of importance.

The Jubilee and the Vigilant reached down along the low, sandy shores toward where, hidden in the summer haze, the lighthouse stood on Point Judith. The tide was running to the eastward. A fleet of steam yachts, keeping at a respectful distance, followed the two racers. At Race Rork the unofficial time of the cup-defenders was as follows: Jubilee, 10:48:35; Vigilant, 10:52:00. After they had passed out onto the open ocean the Jubilee took in her ordinary working staysail and set a balloon staysail. The Vigilant quickly followed her in doing so. Off Noyes Point both yachts set balloon jib-topsails. Off Quonocontaug Beach it was seen that the Vigilant was slowly but surely creeping up on the Boston boat. The gain was hardly perceptible, but still it was a gain, and the hopes of Boston fell as those of New-York rose. It is a "far cry to Lochaber," and it is forty miles from New-London to Newport, so as yet the race might belong to either boat. The wind held steady from the southwest, and the bright sun made the haze which hung about the distant shores a veil of silver shot with golden streaks where the shafts of sunlight broke through. There was scarcely a ripple on the water. Even the long ocean swells seemed scarcely to move themselves, and down the broad and shining way the great fleet swam, led by the towering sloops.

Boston men would not believe their eyes as slowly but surely the powerful Vigilant, with her immense weight of lead and her great displacement, drew up on the Jubilee. They laid it fo a change in the position in their points of observation. When Point Judith was reached, however, all doubt ceased even in the minds of those who are privileged to live under the shadow of the gilded dome. Then they sincerely regretted the act of banishment against Roger Williams, for they saw that the sloop built in Rhode Island was nearly up to the hope of Boston. As the point was rounded it was seen that the Vigilant was lapping on to the Jubilee's quarter, and as they shaped their course more northerly and set their great spinnakers it was seen that the Vigilant was trying to blanket the Jubilee, for she held the windward position and was taking all the advantage which it offered her. The two yachts passed Point Judith as follows: Jubilee, 1:41:19; Vigilant, 1:41:58. Then began the most exciting part of the race. The Vigilant would draw up on the weather side of the Jubilee and the Boston boat's sails would shake as the wind was taken out of her canvas. The Herreshoff boat tried to pass her antagonist again and again, but with no satisfactory results. Finally it seemed as if the Vigilant remembered that she was getting into Rhode Island waters, and with a burst of speed, for which there was apparently nothing to account, she moved ahead of her rival and led her up the entrance of Narragansett Bay to the finish.

As the two big cup defenders swept up toward Fort Dumpling the cup-defender Pilgrim was seen standing out. She made a most beautiful appearance. Her sails were, in cut and set, superior to those of any of the other cup-defenders, and if one could forget that she drew twenty feet of

water and had little under water except a wedge of steel and lead, a yachtsman would fall in love with her.

The winners in the various classes were Constellation, Fortuna, Lasca, Neaera, Vigilant, Katrina, Queen Mab, Eclipse, Wasp and Mariquita. The time of the race was as follows:

SCHOONERS—CLASS 1.

Name.	Start. H. M. S.	Fin'sh. H. M. S.	Elapsed Time. H. M. S.	Corrected Time. H. M. S.
Dauntless	10:25:00	4:12:27	5:47:27	5:47:27
Constellation	10:25:00	3:47:51	5:22:54	5:20:54
Yampa	10:25:00	4:10:44	5:3:41	5:52:18
Ramona	10:25:00	4:5:5	5:40:31	5:47:45
Fleetwing	10:25:00	4:13:50	6:18:50	6:13:09
Fo tuna	10:25:00	4:10:12	5:5:1	5:51:12
Montauk	10:25:00	4:40:08	6:15:08	....

SCHOONERS—CLASS 2.

Volunteer	10:25:00	4:10:04	5:45:34	....
Lasca	10:21:00	3:34:11	5:13:11	5:11:48
Alcaea	10:25:00	4:25:28	6:10:28	....
Mayflower	10:22:10	3:51:43	5:10:03	5:25:37
Emerald	10:23:02	4:10:10	5:14:40	5:3:9
Atlantic	10:25:00	4:25:40	0:00:10	5:54:25
Marguerite	10:24:52	4:21:01	5:56:09	5:50:09
Ariel	10:11:45	3:45:50	5:24:15	5:27:13
Dacm'r	10:23:37	4:20:15	6:02:30	5:55:31
Shamrock	10:25:00	4:25:00	5:00:18	5:52:32

SCHOONERS—CLASS 5.

	H. M. S.	H. M. S.	H. M. S.	H. M. S.
Gevella	10:25:00	4:58:56	6:33:56	6:35:46
Loyal	10:25:00	4:57:58	6:32:58	....
Neaera	10:24:21	4:50:15	6:25:54	6:22:30

SLOOPS—CLASS 1.

| Jubilee | 10:10:00 | 3:12:52 | 5:02:52 | .... |
| Vigilant | 10:10:00 | 3:11:41 | 5:01:41 | .... |

SLOOPS—CLASS 3.

Katrina	10:16:42	3:51:51	5:35:09	5:35:09
Gracie	10:10:10	4:33:13	6:14:03	6:12:06
Bedouin	10:17:27	4:19:21	6:01:54	5:59:00
Huron	10:16:55	4:02:40	5:46:08	5:38:36

SLOOPS—CLASS 4.

Wayward	10:20:00	4:14:21	6:24:21	6:24:21
Hildegarde	10:16:24	4:17:73	6:00:49	6:00:35
Queen Mab	10:18:54	4:23:24	6:04:30	5:50:31

SLOOPS—CLASS 5.

| Eclipse | 10:20:00 | 5:01:56 | 6:41:56 | 6:41:56 |
| Clara | 10:20:00 | 5:04:44 | 6:44:44 | 6:44:35 |

SLOOPS—CLASS 6.

Wasp	10:18:00	3:53:19	5:35:19	5:35:19
Jessica	10:18:49	4:40:57	6:28:02	6:20:29
Carmita	10:20:00	4:44:21	6:24:21	....
Vvira	10:16:08	4:31:14	6:15:06	6:02:03

SLOOPS—CLASS 7.

Mariquita	10:18:40	4:40:08	6:21:28	6:21:28
Bonnie Kate	10:18:00	......	......	......
Rosalind	10:20:10	......	......	......
Nymph	10:18:24	4:57:44	6:38:50	....

The Lasca sailed, as she has all through the cruise, in excellent form, and is doing much better than she did last year. The Constellation is out for prizes this season and so far she has got them. She was, of course a winner to-day.

After the race General Paine said: "I am perfectly satisfied with what the Jubilee has done to-day, and I believe that were the yachts officially measured we will be found to have won the race. The Jubilee steers easily and her speed is most satisfactory."

C. Oliver Iselin, who was aboard the Vigilant, said: "I am perfectly satisfied with the Vigilant and of the opinion that we won the race. The Vigilant is a most speedy boat and has not yet shown what she can do. I am confident that, even with our loss at the start ,and with the time allowance which we may have to allow the Jubilee, that we won to-day's race."

The Colonia came on here, it seems, to have a new bowsprit and shrouds put on her before she sailed in the Goelet Cup races. All day to-day men were at work on her who had been sent down from Bristol by the Herreshoffs. Among those working on her was Archibald Rogers, divested of coat and waist-coat, and doing two men's work.

Governor Russell, of Massachusetts, arrived here from Boston to-day and went aboard the Constellation where he will be a guest of Bayard Thayer for the rest of the cruise.

To-night Commodore Morgan gave a reception at his house at Beacon Rock to the yachtsmen of the fleet. The reception was from 9 to 11 o'clock, and the May, brilliant with lights, was anchored in the cove in front of the house.

IN FOGS AND CALMS.

THE RACE FOR THE GOELET CUPS OFF NEWPORT A FAILURE.

THOUSANDS GO OUT TO SEE THE CONTEST AND RETURN DISHEARTENED—THE PILGRIM DISAPPOINTS HER ADMIRERS—IT STILL LOOKS LIKE THE VIGILANT AND JUBILEE — YACHTSMEN SIGH FOR OCEAN BREEZES TO-DAY.

(BY TELEGRAPH TO THE TRIBUNE.)

Newport, R. I., Aug. 11.—Fog and a plentiful lack of wind made the race for the Goelet cups a failure to-day. Though the four cup defenders—Vigilant, Jubilee, Colonia and Pilgrim—started in the race, and though enough people went out to see the run to make a good-sized city, the breezes of the ocean would not blow, and the yachts drifted over the Vineyard Sound and Hen and Chickens course in a manner which made all who saw them wish for power to command the elements and summer breezes from the vasty deep. The race proved nothing and meant, if possible, less than nothing. When the flagship May steamed out of the harbor at 10 o'clock the wind was blowing lightly from the northwest and there was every prospect of a good race. But high up in the sky were watery looking clouds, evidently the remnants of the fog which the night before had shut down upon Newport, and those who are weather wise in this locality shook their heads when they looked at them. Their fears proved to be well founded, for before the race was over the fog came down, first in great bands of obscurity through which the racing yachts felt their way, and finally in a blanket which blotted out sea and land, leaving the racing fleet to finish in the darkness of a foggy night, and nights that are foggy are dense, impenetrable and unprofitable here in Newport.

If the race of to-day could be said to give any clew as to which of the four cup defenders is the fleetest and is destined to defend the America's Cup, it might be said that the palm lies between the Vigilant and the Jubilee, with a possibility of the Colonia. These three yachts sailed a race, if race it could be called, which showed that they were at least good drifters. The Colonia especially did good work, and while in the first part of the race she was not supposed to have any show for the victory she came up on the Vigilant and Jubilee at the Vineyard Sound lightship and cheered the hearts of those who believe in her and in the principles upon which she is constructed. As it was in yesterday's race so it was to-day, the question of the victory among the cup defenders lying between the Vigilant and the Jubilee. To-day the uncertainty of the victory was because the winds slept in their ocean caves and night and fog had settled down upon the Narragansett shore before the yachts finished. Yesterday it was because they had not been measured and no man knew the time allowance. No one will probably know the time allowance between the cup defenders until the international races are sailed.

The Pilgrim was a great disappointment to her friends to-day. She is such a pretty looking boat and has done so well in her sailing about the coast that she had a large following of yachtsmen who saw the constellations rise and set on her. She broke the clew to her club topsail when she started yesterday, and could not carry that sail, but that did not account for the poor showing she made in the race.

A big fleet of steamers and yachts poured out of the harbor after the flagship May in the morning and a great floating city was about the yellow hull of the lightship which rocks on Brenton's Reef when the starting signal was given at 11:35. The sloops were manœuvring for position and when the gun from the May announced that the race was begun the Jubilee and Vigilant were near the line. The Vigilant had Nathaniel Herreshoff on board, but she was out-manoeuvred by the Paine boat Jubilee and crossed the line astern of the Boston craft. The order of the start was as follows: Jubilee, Vigilant, Colonia, Pilgrim, Ilderim, Lasca, Ariel, Volunteer, Emerald, Marguerite, Mayflower, Constellation, Dagmar and Loyal.

The Pilgrim broke her club topsail yard before she crossed the line and had to set a working topsail. Then the yachts reached out for the entrance of Vineyard Sound, the schooners following far behind, and all the other sloops, except the cup-defenders, were with them. Soon after the line was crossed the Vigilant tacked and got to the windward of the Jubilee. She apparently held the winning position. When she came about again on the port tack every one thought that the race was hers. But winds are fickle even when they blow lightly, and before the Vineyard Haven Lightship was reached the faint and dying ghost of a breeze had shifted to southeast, thus putting the Jubilee in the windward position.

The Colonia was laying along astern of the leaders. As to the Pilgrim, she was so hopelessly in the "ruck" that she came on the starboard tack and went hunting luck over toward the shore. The lateness of the time of starting the race could not have had anything to do with the lack of wind, but it has been an unfortunate coincidence that on this cruise winds have refused to blow, and the races have been started late. Commodore Morgan does not seem to have the command over the elements as did his predecessor, Commodore Gerry, who used to rejoice in "Commodore's weather." The Volunteer led the schooners and also most of the sloops.

The cup defenders opened for themselves a great space between the fleet and themselves. Great bands of fog lay across the pathway of the fleet and the yachts pushed through them every now and then. The Vineyard Sound lightship was reached by the leading boats when there was every indication of a flat calm, and soon after the calm came upon the waters. It is idle to tell of the rest of the race, for of the thousands who went out to view it no man saw it. The Hen and Chickens was passed with the Jubilee still ahead and the Vigilant close to her. The Colonia was crawling up. Spinnakers and balloon-jibtopsails were set to catch every bit of breeze which wandered over the waters. Of the schooners the Volunteer was still ahead. Then fog and night came down upon the ocean, and the great fleet of steam yachts, tugs and excursion steamers turned back to Newport. The May went to Brenton's Reef and waited in the gloom and the darkness for the yachts to come in. At midnight she was still out there. It was a most disappointing attempt to sail a race.

Among the large fleet of steam yachts which followed over the course to-day was the Senator, the property of William H. Crane, the comedian. Flying from the topmast of the yacht was the State flag of Massachusetts, Governor Russell being one of Mr. Crane's guests. In the forenoon the Governor was taken off the schooner yacht Constellation, on which he was a guest, by Mr. Crane, and during the race he was one of the interested spectators. Among Mr. Crane's other guests were Governor Russell's brother, Colonel Russell; Eugene H. Lewis and T. O'Brien. After the race the party dined at the Casino.

VIGILANT WITHOUT A RIVAL.

COMPLETE TRIUMPH OF THE CENTREBOARD OVER THE KEEL BOATS.

HERRESHOFF STILL THE WORLD'S GREATEST
NAVAL ARCHITECT—A GRAND RACE OF THE
CUP-DEFENDERS OVER THIRTY MILES
OF ROLLING SEA—THE JUBILEE
SECOND—A DISCREDITED
PILGRIM.

[BY TELEGRAPH TO THE TRIBUNE.]

Newport, R. I., Aug. 17.—The yacht which in all probability is to defend the America's Cup, sprang forth to-day over thirty miles of rolling water, and powerful and swift, proved her superiority over her competitors. Last night all four of the cup-defenders had their following. To-night there is the name of but one boat on men's tongues, and the name is Vigilant. Her performance was as wonderful as her prowess has been great. Her victory was overwhelming and conclusive. In windward work, in running, in carrying her sail, in every quality which goes to make up the excellence of a racing yacht, the Vigilant showed herself masterful and great. The other boats are swift—swifter than anything ever before seen on this side of the water—but their speed was as the gentle zephyr compared with a whirlwind to hers. They have weatherly qualities and good points of sailing, but they are as moons before the sun to those of the Vigilant. The Boston fin-keels, which have heretofore been looked upon as possessing remarkable speed, whatever might be said regarding their type as boats, were no more a match for her than as if they had never been built. The Colonia, too, was a disappointment to those who believe in keel boats, and found the only competitor with which she had any chance of winning in the Paine boat Jubilee. The American mind, whether it knows anything about the subject or not, clings tenaciously to the centreboard. For so many years has the American centreboard defeated the British keel that it has become to the popular minds almost one of the palladiums of our liberties, and so it will be read with universal satisfaction throughout the land that to-day, in a fair trial, in a fleet which could scarcely have been more thorough, the centreboard Vigilant overwhelmingly defeated the keel-boat Colonia, and the fin-keels of Boston. It might be beneficial to American yachting some day to have the prejudice against keel-boats swept away, but as long as such centreboard boats as the Vigilant can be built it never will be. In the light of her performances to-day, even such a suggestion sounds like the piping of a broken reed alongside the victorious pealing of an organ.

Sorrow sits among the yachtsmen of Boston. Their Jubilee has turned to sorrow and the Pilgrim wanders forlorn and forsaken. Great still is Herreshoff, and the blind old man, who, in a rocking boat, with sightless eyes turned over toward the racers following them over the course, stands before the world its greatest naval architect. It was something pathetic that at the finish the scales could not have for an instant been lifted from his eyes and he could have caught a vision of his handiwork sweeping in power and victory across the line. All through the cruise the Vigilant had been gaining in favor and to-day she put all doubts at rest. The trial races will be sailed of course. They must be, but who that saw the race to-day, the rushing winds, the tossing waves and struggling yachts

can have any doubt of the result? As to the Valkyrie, she must have the speed of the wind and the power of the sea if she can defeat the Vigilant. Never before have the cup-defenders been brought together in a race when their qualities could be tested. To-day their battle-ground was the open ocean, and wind and sea combined to make their struggle one long to be remembered. It was the first of the series for the Astor cups, the two beautiful trophies made by Tiffany & Co., and the winds, which have slept in their ocean caves during the cruise, were loosed upon the sea. All four of the yachts—the cup-defenders were the only entries—had been put in perfect condition for the race and nothing was wanting to make it a success.

The wind blew a twenty-knot breeze from the south-southeast, and a great fleet of steam yachts, tugs and excursion steamers gathered about the Brenton's Reef Lightship, waiting impatiently for the start. At 11 o'clock the flagship May was seen steaming down by Fort Dumpling, and soon after she had taken up a position off the lightship. She ran up at her fore signals that the cruise would be fifteen miles south-southeast and return. Then away into the obscurity of the horizon's rim steamed the tug Scandinavian to drop over the buoy whose fluttering red flag should mark the end of the outward run of the cruise. The sky was heavy with clouds, and the sea was every minute getting higher, its dull surface sprinkled about with white caps and its edges gleaming, ragged and white, up to the high rocks of the shore, "like a banner torn with flying on a wild steed's flying mane." Ensigns and signals of the many yachts were patches of bright color against the sombre background of the sea and the sky, and over the sullen sea, under the lowering sky, through the waiting fleet the four great white ghosts of cup-defenders glided about, waiting for the starting signal. They were all so majestic of motion, so graceful of form, so towering and splendid in the beat of their great white wings that victory might seem perched on the mast of any one of them. At 11:25 a gun was fired from the May as a preparatory signal. The experts at the helms of the four boats knew that in ten minutes the starting signal would be given, and began to manoeuvre for position. So well did they time it that when, at 11:35, a bright red ball was run up on the triadic stay of the May and a gun spoke from her side they were all close to the line, and were over it in less than a minute. The Jubilee was over first at 11:35:21. The Pilgrim was five seconds behind her, and the Colonia was 32 seconds behind the Pilgrim. The Vigilant was the last boat over. She crossed 26 seconds behind the Colonia. The yachts were on the starboard tack, and all had up small jib-topsails and club-topsails except the Jubilee, which did not carry any jib-topsail. The Vigilant was to windward, with the Colonia next, the Pilgrim to leeward of her and the Jubilee to windward of the fleet.

Soon after the yachts crossed the Vigilant headed up, working for a more windward position. She pointed wonderfully, and footed as well as she pointed. All of her good qualities came to the front at once and were never again out of sight while the race was on. The yachts made a long leg to the eastward on the starboard tack. The Pilgrim was ahead, but to leeward; then came the Jubilee, the Colonia and Vigilant, each boat holding a more windward position than the one ahead of it. The flood tide was running strong up into Seaconnet River, and it set the leading boats well up to the northward. The Pilgrim soon saw that this would never do. She was not only getting hopelessly to leeward, but the other boats were outfooting her.

She resolved on a bold move, and at 11:50 came about on the port tack and stood to the westward. If the wind had hauled to the westward it might have helped her, but it did not, nor was there at any time any prospect of it. A favorable shift of wind might have helped her, but it could never have saved the day for her, and it is doubtful if Mr. Stewart or Mr. Palmer would care to win such a barren victory as one caused by a "fluke." So the Pilgrim wandered out into the misty west, further and further away from the other boats, which held their tack still when the Pilgrim was getting hull down over toward Block Island. The Jubilee, Colonia and Vigilant were now near together, but the Vigilant was not only to windward, but also ahead of them. It was evident she was going to show the way over the course, but it was also evident that she would not do so without a supreme struggle on the part of her flying antagonists. There could be no criticism of the way the yachts were handled. The best talent to be had was on board of them and all that human skill and human experience and the indefinable genius which makes a man a great yacht sailor was exercised to the full in the handling of the sloops upon whose contest the eyes of the maritime world were fixed. The yachts themselves, their sails and spars and rigging, seemed alive and sentient as they struggled over the windswept sea.

At 12:09 the Colonia came about. She was followed a minute later by the Vigilant, and a minute and a half after her the Jubilee also came on the port tack. The Colonia reached through the lee of the Vigilant, but so far to leeward that it was of no benefit to her, and her burst of speed was more than equalled by the Vigilant, which at once began to outfoot her, still pointing high in the wind. The Colonia could not carry her jib-topsail any longer, and took it in. The Jubilee also took in hers, leaving the Vigilant the only boat with a jib-topsail set. At 12:39 the Vigilant followed the example of the Colonia and Jubilee, and took her jib-topsail in. The three yachts stood away down toward where the Pilgrim was still holding her port back, and it was evident that when they came about their relative positions could be well judged. The wind now shifted from south-southeast to southeast, the change being to the disadvantage of the Pilgrim. It was not enough to her disadvantage, as even her most enthusiastic admirers admit to-night, to account for her humiliating defeat. At 12:55 the Pilgrim came about on the starboard tack and passed astern of the Vigilant. The Vigilant came on the starboard tack and crossed the bows of the Pilgrim. The Colonia came on the starboard tack at 1:16. At 1:20 the Vigilant came on the port tack. The Vigilant, Pilgrim and Jubilee were now on the port tack and the Colonia on the starboard tack. The Colonia went astern of the Pilgrim at 1:23 and came about on the port tack. She weathered the Pilgrim in doing it. At 1:28 the Pilgrim was about again, followed by the Vigilant two minutes later. Every tack showed that the Vigilant was rapidly gaining and that the Pilgrim was losing.

So the yachts worked their way out toward the red flag fluttering on that rolling water, and the race resolved itself down to a struggle for second place between the Jubilee and Colonia. Finally, after a few more tacks, all four of the great sloops came rushing down on the starboard tack for the mark. The majestic Vigilant, far in advance of the others, stood on by the mark and then, calculating the distance to a nicety, came on the port tack and rounded, jibing her bow over to port as she did so. The Colonia and Jubilee came down to the

mark together, the Jubilee a little in the lead. Minutes astern of them came the Pilgrim, struggling hard in a hopeless race. They all jibed around and set their spinnakers as soon as they could after rounding. The time of the yachts at the outer mark was as follows:

Names.	Time.	Names.	Time.
Vigilant	2:06:37	Colonia	2:13:15
Jubilee	2:12:20	Pilgrim	2:16:42

The Vigilant got her spinnaker set five minutes after rounding the mark. The Jubilee set hers at 2:12:25, and Colonia flung her great silk spinnaker to the winds in short order. The Pilgrim also got her spinnaker out in good season, and away the great boats flew for home and Brenton's Reef, for defeat and victory. The Vigilant had been splendid on the wind, she was magnificent off of it. She flew further and further away, and the others followed. The wind had lulled a little just before the outer mark was reached and the rain had fallen in torrents, but nobody cared for the rain, though all were anxious about the wind. But there was no cause for anxiety, for soon after the outer mark was rounded the wind freshened again, and kept on increasing until, when the finish was neared, it was blowing half a gale and a heavy sea was running. The Colonia and Jubilee had a good race of it all the way home, and when about half the distance was run it looked as if the Colonia might take second place. She could not do it, however, and the Jubilee remained ahead of her till the finish. When the Pilgrim had run an hour's time in from the outer mark she carried away the jaws of her gaff. This put her entirely out of a race in which she never from the start had a chance of victory. She took in her great spinnaker and her balloon jib-topsail, and stood off to the eastward, where a tug picked her up and towed her back to port, a forlorn and discredited boat. The rain was still falling when the Vigilant, with a great rush, crossed the line, and in the rain and wind and howling sea she achieved a splendid victory. Minutes behind her came the Jubilee and Colonia, and the race was over. The time of the race was as follows:

Jubilee	11:35:21	3:13:34	4:08:13
Pilgrim	11:35:26	Not timed.	
Colonia	11:35:58	3:44:19	4:08:21
Vigilant	11:36:19	3:39:11	4:02:52

The Vigilant beat the Jubilee to the outer mark by 7 minutes and 43 seconds. She beat the Colonia by 8 minutes and 38 seconds, and the Pilgrim by 10 minutes and 5 seconds. The run from home was made by the Vigilant in 1 hour 34 minutes and 34 seconds. The Jubilee made the run in 1 hour 31 minutes and 34 seconds, and the Colonia in 1 hour 31 minutes and 4 seconds. This show at an apparent superiority in running in the other boats is only apparent, for it must be remembered that the wind fell as the yachts approached the outer mark, and that after the Vigilant was well on her way home it came up howling out of the southeast again and the seaward yachts brought it up with them, thus getting a great advantage. Under similar circumstances slow yachts have frequently beaten fast ones, but no vagaries of wind could beat the Vigilant. She lies anchored in the shelter of the harbor to-night, sole and incomparable, a ruler of the waters and their powers.

As the Jubilee was running for the harbor after the race she suffered an accident similar to that which overtook the Pilgrim, and broke the jaws of her gaff.

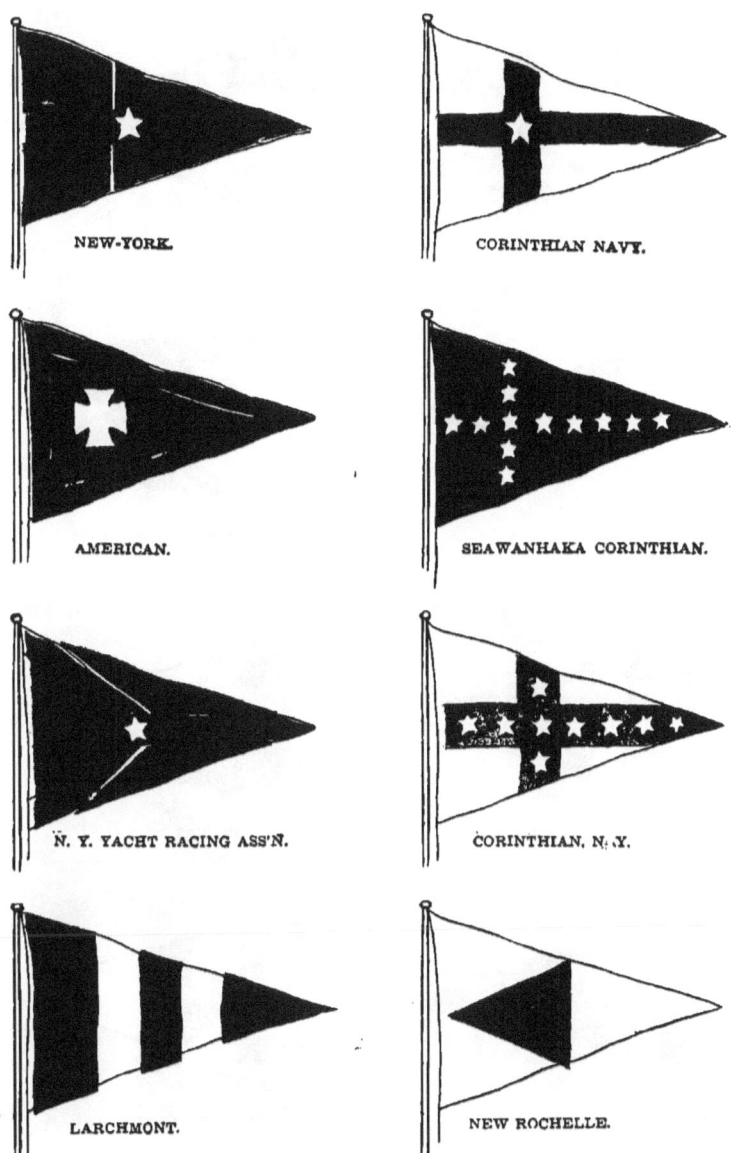

NEW-YORK.

CORINTHIAN NAVY.

AMERICAN.

SEAWANHAKA CORINTHIAN.

N. Y. YACHT RACING ASS'N.

CORINTHIAN, N. Y.

LARCHMONT.

NEW ROCHELLE.

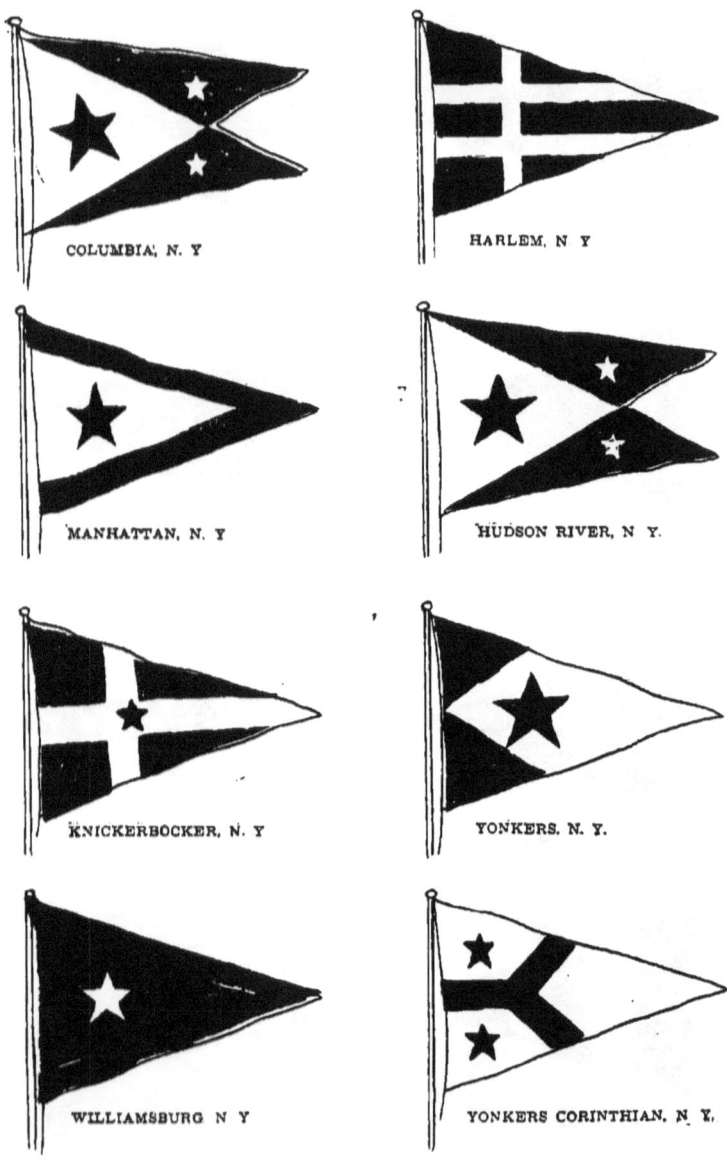

COLUMBIA, N. Y

HARLEM, N. Y

MANHATTAN, N. Y

HUDSON RIVER, N. Y.

KNICKERBOCKER, N. Y

YONKERS, N. Y.

WILLIAMSBURG N Y

YONKERS CORINTHIAN, N. Y.

ATLANTIC. Brooklyn.

HEMPSTEAD BAY, N Y.

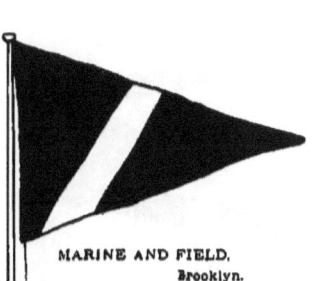

BROOKLYN. Brooklyn.

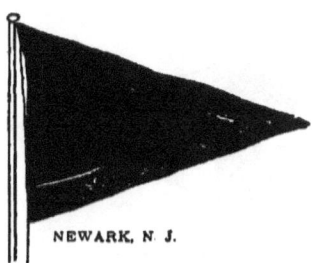

NEWARK, N. J.

MARINE AND FIELD,
Brooklyn.

NEW JERSEY,
Hoboken, N. J

JAMAICA BAY

JERSEY CITY, N. J.

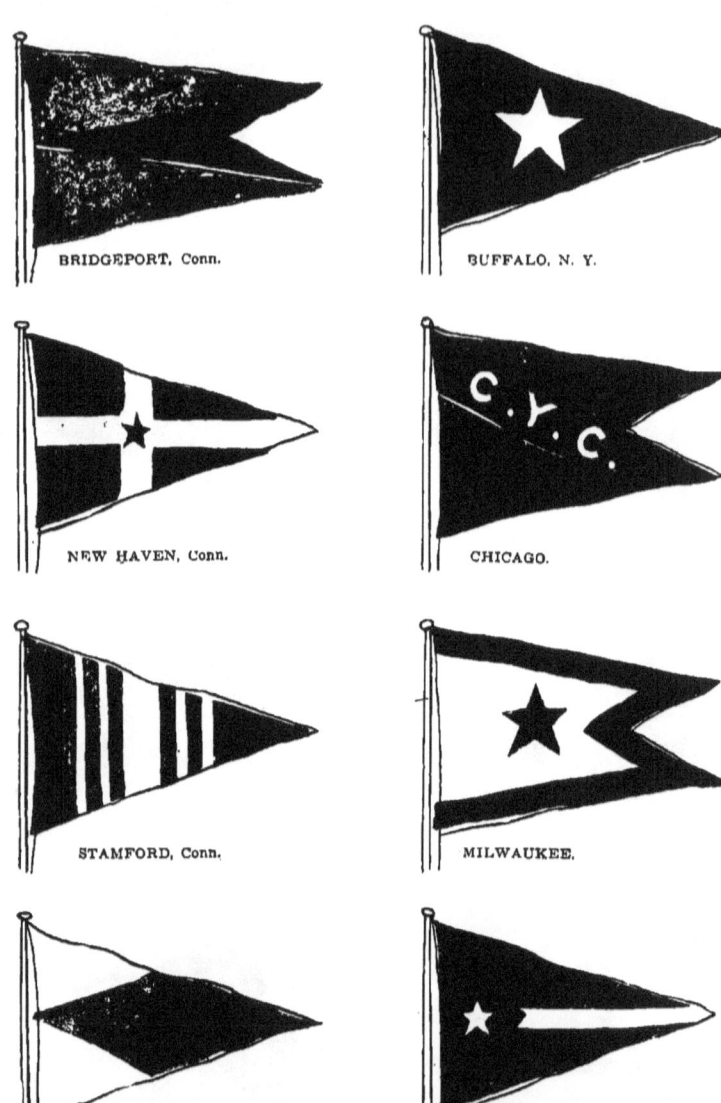

BRIDGEPORT, Conn.

BUFFALO, N. Y.

NEW HAVEN, Conn.

CHICAGO.

STAMFORD, Conn.

MILWAUKEE.

INDIAN HARBOR.

SAN FRANCISCO.

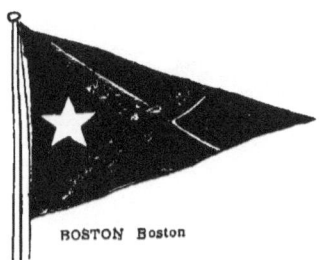

BOSTON Boston

EASTERN,
Marblehead, Mass.

ATLANTIC, Boston.

HULL CORINTHIAN, Mass.

MASSACHUSETTS,

HAVERHILL, Mass.

SOUTH BOSTON.

COMMONWEALTH,
South Boston.

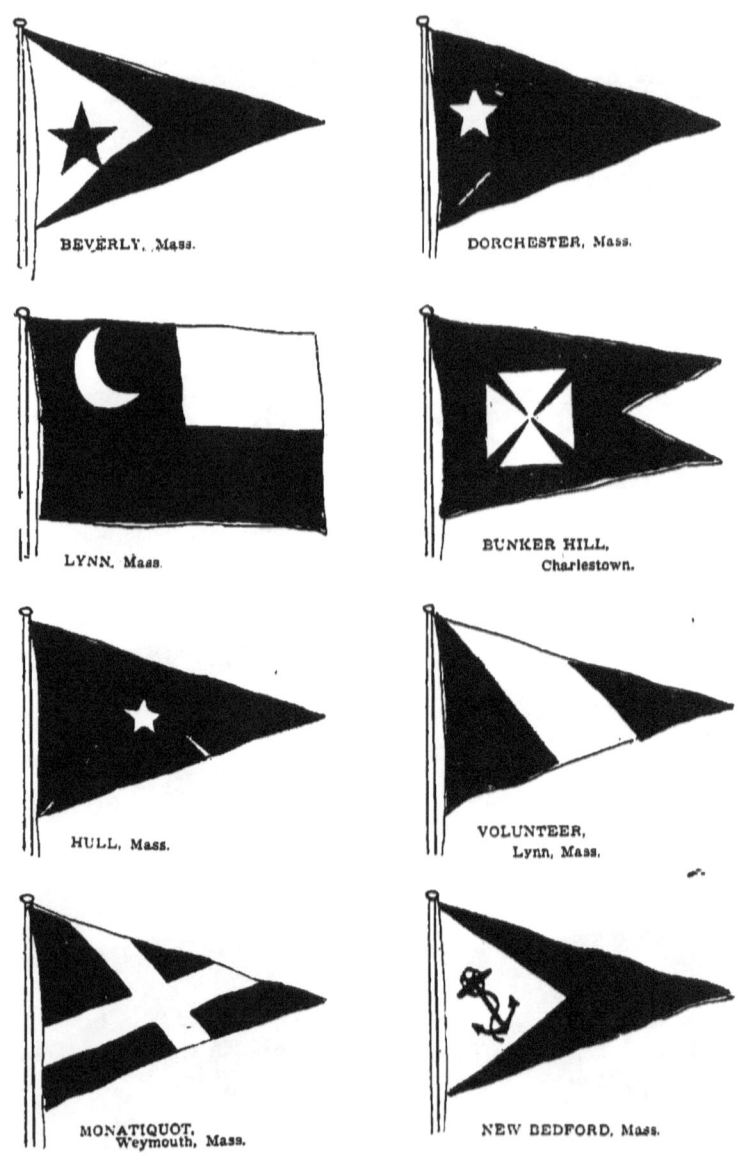

BEVERLY, Mass.

DORCHESTER, Mass.

LYNN, Mass.

BUNKER HILL,
Charlestown.

HULL, Mass.

VOLUNTEER,
Lynn, Mass.

MONATIQUOT,
Weymouth, Mass.

NEW BEDFORD, Mass.

AMERICAN,
NEWBURYPORT. Mass.

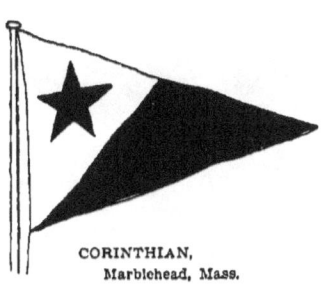

CORINTHIAN,
Marblehead, Mass.

CAPE ANN. Mass.

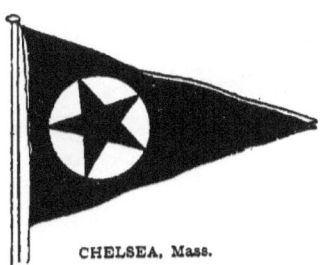

CHELSEA, Mass.

WEST LYNN, Mass.

JEFFRIES,
East Boston.

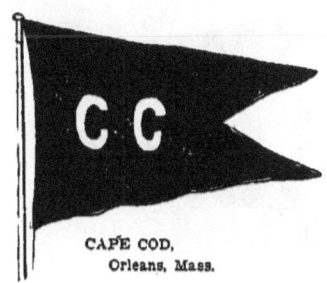

CAPE COD,
Orleans, Mass.

FALL RIVER.

CLEVELAND, Ohio.

MOBILE. Ala.

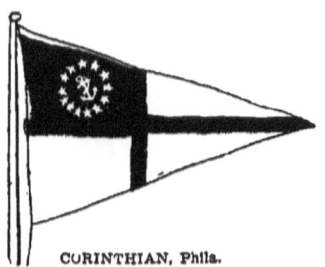

CORINTHIAN, Phila.

SOUTHERN,
Lake Pontchartrain.

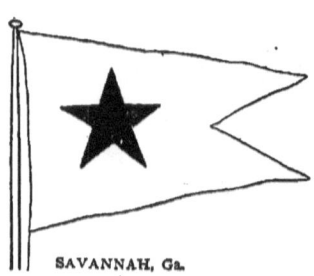

SAVANNAH, Ga.

ST. AUGUSTINE, Fla.

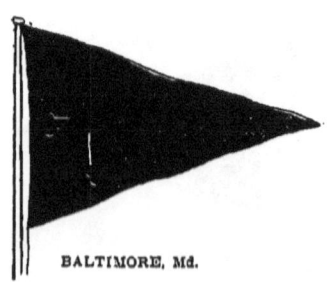

BALTIMORE, Md.

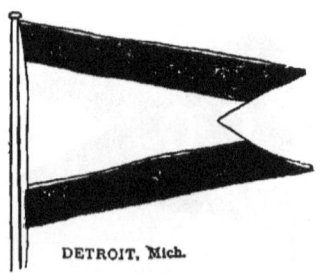

DETROIT, Mich.

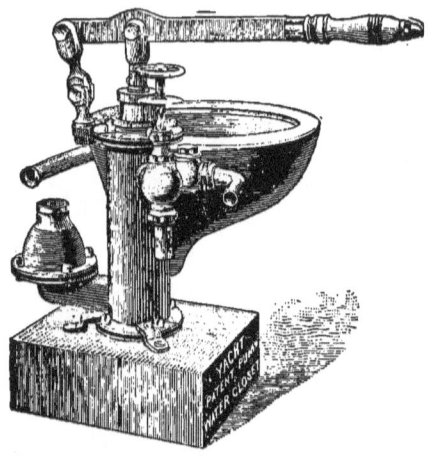

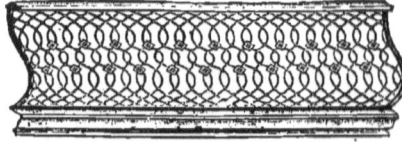

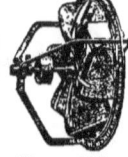

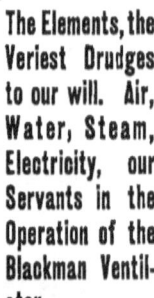

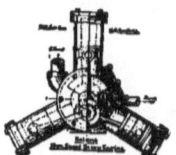

Merritt's Wrecking Organization.

CAPT. ISRAEL J. MERRITT, and his son, Mr. Israel J. Merritt, Jr., are the sole owners of this great concern. It is the largest and most successful house in the world engaged in the wrecking business. Besides their Main Office at 49 Wall Street, New York, and a large Storehouse and Docks at Stapleton, Staten Island, they have Offices, Storehouse and Docks at Norfolk, Va., and are permanently stationed there, and own a fleet of Steamers, Sailing Vessels and Pontoons, specially built, rigged and fitted out, regardless of cost, for the work. They have 30 steam pumps and boilers—all portable—capable of throwing from 20 to 70 barrels of water per minute ; 20 manilla cables, 14 to 20 inches in circumference, each 200 fathoms long; 26 large wrecking anchors, hoisting machinery, and numerous tools for handling wrecked cargoes.

Their resources are perfect and complete. They do nearly all the heavy wrecking on the Atlantic coast, and confine themselves strictly to the business of wrecking, employing from 150 to 250 men, including the most skillful divers, trained men and mechanics, and have accomplished the work of saving the most difficult cases known. Their offices are open night and day, so that no time is lost when the news of a wreck arrives. Experience,

enterprise, and energy, coupled with a perfect equipment, have placed them far in the lead in their line of business. Capt. Merritt, who can justly claim the honor of being the pioneer wrecker, having served thirty-five years with the Underwriters and the Coast Wrecking Company as a manager, established the present organization in 1880.

To ship owners and underwriters the utility of this organization is incalculable.

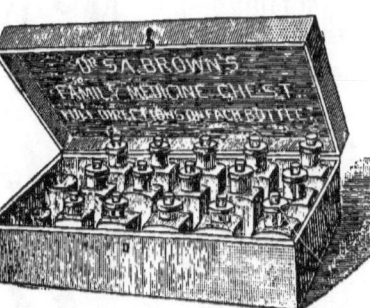

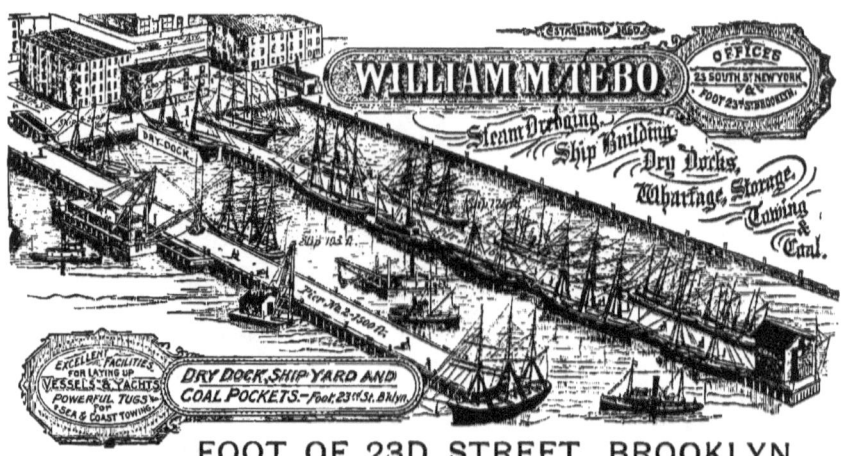

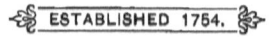

Tripple Expansion Engines for Auxiliary Steam Yacht "Wild Duck," built by The Atlantic Works, for Hon. John M. Forbes.

ESTABLISHED IN 1853.

The Atlantic Works,

Border, Maverick, and New Sts.,

Docks Opposite the Navy Yard.   EAST BOSTON, MASS.

————— BUILDERS OF —————

Steamships, Tow Boats, Steam Yachts,

In STEEL, IRON or WOOD.

Marine Engines, Boilers and Tanks.

COPPERSMITH WORK and GENERAL REPAIRING.

MARINE RAILWAY.

EXCELS ALL! EXCELS ALL!!

Bottled by the Distillers

AFTER YEARS OF CAREFUL MATURING.

ASK FOR IT

AT

YOUR GROCERS.

ALLOW NO

SUBSTITUTE.

PURITY

GUARANTEED

—BY THE—

ZENO

DISTILLERY CO.

FOR SALE WHOLESALE.

PHELAN & DUVAL, 22 South William Street, New York.
ARNETT G. SMITH, 14 Fulton Street, New York.
F. BOEGLER & CO., 26 South William Street, New York.
BLANCHARD, FARRAR & CO., 14-15 Dock Square, Boston, Mass.
JOSEPH THOMPSON, 21-23 Decatur Street, Atlanta, Ga.
G. C. & H. C. BUTCHER, 100-102 Fulton Street, Brooklyn.
H. A. GRAEF'S SON, 40 Court Street, Brooklyn.

And numerous other First-class Dealers throughout the United States

EASTERN OFFICE:

16 South William Street, New York City.

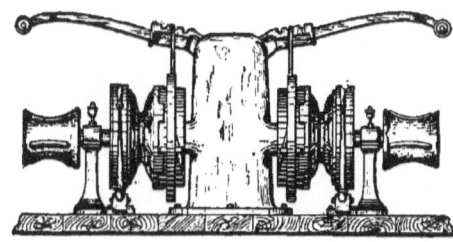

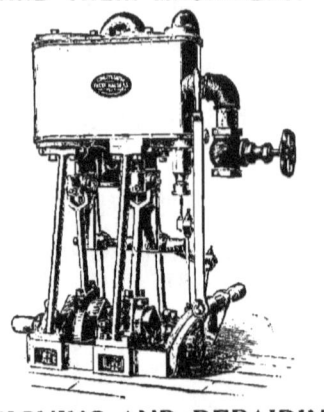

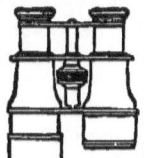

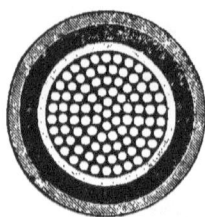 

BISHOP GUTTA=PERCHA CO.,

MANUFACTURERS OF

Telegraph Cables,

Insulated Wires and Gutta-Percha Goods,

420 to 426 EAST 25th ST.,

New York.

INSULATED WIRES and CABLES of Highest Grade for MARINE WORK; under water, under ground, or under any conditions. All the cables used by the Light House Department for lighting Electric Buoys —and most of those used by the Life Saving, Weather Bureau, Signal Service and other Government Departments have been devised and made by this Company and we confidently refer to the Electrical Experts of every department at Washington as well as to those of our several technical schools.

"This wire also showed no deterioration from exposure to moist air, fresh plaster, damp earth, etc., after several months exposure. Its insulating power also was unaffected by a like exposure to illuminating gas."

(Signed), HENRY MORTON.

ANNAPOLIS, MD., February 15th, 1889.

DEAR SIR:—I send you herewith a report of the tests of the four samples of electric light wires you sent me for examination. Desiring to find out as much as possible about wires for ships, I have taken advantage of your permission to subject these samples to severe tests and have no fault to find with them.

(Signed), N. M. TERRY,
Professor of Physics.

ELECTRIC BUOYS LIGHTED BY BISHOP CABLES.

We claim to make only the best.
We do not try to make cheap grades.
Everything guaranteed as represented.

HENRY A. REED,

Treasurer and Manager.